MW00944363

Freshman
Season

How I Dodged and Tackled High School

MARY MARINO

INFINITY
PUBLISHING.COM

Copyright © 2009 by Mary Marino

All rights reserved. No part of this book shall be reproduced or transmitted in any form or by any means, electronic, mechanical, magnetic, photographic including photocopying, recording or by any information storage and retrieval system, without prior written permission of the publisher. No patent liability is assumed with respect to the use of the information contained herein. Although every precaution has been taken in the preparation of this book, the publisher and author assume no responsibility for errors or omissions. Neither is any liability assumed for damages resulting from the use of the information contained herein.

This is a work of fiction. Names, characters, places, and incidents either are the product of the author's imagination or are used fictitiously. Any resemblance to actual events or locales or persons, living or dead, is entirely coincidental.

ISBN 0-7414-5537-4

Published by:

PUBLISHING.COM

1094 New DeHaven Street, Suite 100
West Conshohocken, PA 19428-2713
Info@buybooksontheweb.com
www.buybooksontheweb.com
Toll-free (877) BUY BOOK
Local Phone (610) 941-9999
Fax (610) 941-9959

Printed in the United States of America

Published March 2010

For every girl

who picked up

a hockey stick

and

couldn't put it down.

Preface

I wish there had been a fortune teller at my eighth grade graduation. If I could have peered into her crystal ball and seen the future, I wouldn't have been in such a rush to walk off that stage and start my summer vacation. Honestly, if I had known what was coming, I would have totally asked her to make time stand still. But she probably would have said, "Sorry, kid, no can do; you need to get going. Freezing the clock is not my thing."

I cranked up the volume on my iPod, the music's driving rhythm in perfect sync with my pounding feet. It was about the only thing keeping me going. My usual energy had disappeared a few blocks back, and the sweat dripping down my face was blurring my vision. Browman's Hill was always tough, but never like this. I had to keep pushing to finish, and it wasn't the first time I wished I'd done my running in the morning. *What was I thinking, waiting until the hottest part of the day?*

I could see the top of the hill. Not much more, almost there. I glanced at my watch, and saw nothing but zeroes. *No, Jackie! How could you be so stupid?* I had forgotten to start my watch again; I didn't know my time. I stopped running, clasped my hands over my head, and tried walking off my frustration.

The time on my run today didn't have to be written down or anything, but knowing what I could do was super important to me. It was all about making the team.

All summer, I'd been doing the coach's training program, trying to get my time down in the mile run. Every freshmen field hockey player had to be able to do the mile in

1

less than eight minutes on the first day of practice, so my goal was to beat this time by a whole minute and then some. I figured a good time could be the best way to impress my new coach.

My eyes were still stinging from the sweat. Wiping my face with the bottom of my tank top didn't seem to help much, and I had to keep pacing around so my legs didn't tighten up. I had to admit it. Mom was right. I **was** a scatter-brain for forgetting and now it was costing me. *Dumb, dumb, dumb!*

A couple of deep breaths later, I wandered over to the big oak tree and plopped down to grab some shade. I loved sitting there; it was my favorite spot. From under this tree, my whole world spread out before me, my hometown, Cumberland's Crossing. The town got its name from some general guy who fought in the Revolutionary War or something, so I guess you could say the place was pretty ancient.

Off in the distance was my old school, Washington Elementary. I'd gone there since kindergarten and liked everything about it. Okay, maybe not all the homework. The best part was the playgrounds and ball fields scattered behind the school, where I spent lots of good times playing with my friends.

A breeze started to stir up the late afternoon air and I lifted my face toward the sky to catch it. It got me thinking how it might be cool to have another year at the old school, be the big-shot eighth graders again, but I guessed no one got do-overs.

I shook my head at my goofy thinking. I was probably the only person in the whole freshmen class who had the jitters about going to high school. At my eighth grade graduation, I sure wasn't thinking about the fall. Back then, it was all about summer vacation. Then, a week after graduation, I got this huge manila envelope in the mail. Wham, just like that, everything changed. High school was racing toward me, slamming me right in the face. See, inside the envelope, besides a letter, was a big-time workout program from my new field hockey coach. The letter said there were going to be cuts for the freshman team, so we better be prepared.

Talk about panic attack. You have to understand; for me, playing on the field hockey team was what going to high school was all about. I mean, really, how could it not? Wearing the school colors and charging down the field — that's like life, right? All the rest was just something you put up with 'til you could get to practice. 'Course, parents didn't need to know that stuff, but I had to be honest; that's the way it was for me.

Sitting under the tree, part of the coach's program flashed in my mind, and I tried to picture all the new stretches she wanted us to do. My stomach started rumbling a bit and I swore I could smell my mom's lasagna baking. The anticipation of my favorite dinner was all the motivation I needed to begin my jog back home. The smell got stronger the closer I got to my house, and then it really hit me as I walked in the back door. *Love you, Mom.* Summer barbeque had been getting old lately, so I was glad my mom was up for the change too.

As soon as the back door slammed, Mom called out from the laundry room, "Jackie, set the table for dinner, but not a place for your brother." I rolled my eyes. Like I didn't know where Matt was right now.

The lucky duck had been having soccer practice at the high school for the last two weeks. The varsity hockey girls were there too. I was bummed that freshmen couldn't practice 'til school started, which was really a dumb rule if you asked me.

"And Jackie," she added, "don't forget you have an appointment for a hair cut tomorrow."

I groaned to myself, *forgot about that one.* "Maybe I don't need to go. My hair is fine the way it is," I yelled back. Mom came into the kitchen on that one. I reached up and started smoothing out my traffic-light-red hair that was pulled up into a ponytail. I was hoping that it'd somehow show her that I knew what I was talking about when it came to hair needs.

She smiled sympathetically but still said, "After all that swimming you did this summer, you at least need to get the split ends trimmed."

I saw she was being real persistent, so slipping out of a hair cut was definitely not going to be on the menu. For me, it was going to be one wasted day.

She was rooting around in the fridge when she asked causally, "How about we run out to the mall after dinner?"

I could hear the hope in her voice. She'd been trying this one on me for days. Probably every other girl in town was already there, getting ready for high school. But I knew my mom and I would just tangle over what clothes to pick out, and the fight was **so** not worth it. Besides, she had just won the hair thing. I couldn't concede on everything, so I just handed her one of those no's that meant the discussion was over. She didn't seem too happy with my answer 'cause she.

told me to get upstairs and shower before we sat down to dinner.

Upstairs in my room, the room I shared with my little sister, Lizzie, I took a quick glance around. Lizzie's side of the room was a mix of second-grade pink with all her Barbies and latest Disney idols, while my side was just kind of a mess. I had a few trophies and pictures of my friends on a shelf above my desk, a few inspirational quotes tacked to the wall, but it was all kind of random.

When my sister was born, my brother and I thought she was going to be pretty much something you see after a comma; you know — Matt, Jackie, and the other one. But she turned out to be more of an exclamation point. She could really work it with her flirty ways, batting her eyes and all. My mom ate up the princess routine, so I was kind of glad Lizzie came along. It took some of the girly-girl pressure off of me.

After dinner, I called my two best friends, who happened to be twins, Jules and Tori Hanson. They'd been my best buds ever since the Hanson family moved to town, and we'd been teammates on our school's field hockey and softball teams for the last four years.

When I first met them, it had taken awhile for me to tell them apart. They were both tall and on the thin side but really athletic, with long, dark hair and the same dark brown eyes. Really the only way you could tell them apart was that Tori had a slight dimple when she smiled, which was a lot, while Jules, on the other hand, was way more serious. But I have to say, when it came to someone really standing by you through the tough times or when the sad stuff came along, you could always count on Jules, and that was big deal to me.

Tori answered the phone. "Jackie," she said excitedly, "we only have three more days until school starts."

"I know," I groaned. "I'm not sure if I'm really ready." I was remembering how I had messed up on my run earlier.

"Ready?" said Tori. "Who could not be ready to meet all those cute boys?"

"She means that she doesn't feel ready for hockey to start," her sister, Jules, said from the speaker phone.

"Oh," said Tori. "But, Jackie, of course you're ready; we all are. Look at the tons of running we did. Besides, you are so fast you don't even have to work like the rest of us."

"That's not true," said Jules. "We all have to train the same to be a team, and besides, how do we know that there won't be girls as fast or even faster trying out from the other schools?"

See, besides our school, there were three other schools in the district: Morrisville Middle School, Gibbstown Elementary, and Sacred Heart. That's a lot of girls trying out. Jules going on about a lot of fast players made my stomach lurch a little, and my mind kind of blanked out with the thought.

There was a moment of silence on the phone, but then Jules came through once again and said, "But don't worry, Jackie. We still know you'll be among the best." I smiled to myself. *Jules, you're the greatest.*

"So, are we meeting down at the park tomorrow to practice those stick drills that the coach sent out?" Tori asked.

"Can't," I said. "I have to go with my mom to get my hair cut. I hate going there. The guy always cuts it too short. He never listens."

"Maybe we can have one more practice Wednesday afternoon," Tori said, "and then we can talk about what we are wearing to school on Thursday." We all agreed to this, and the twins wished me luck getting my hair clipped.

Lying in bed that night, there was a lot going on in my head. It wasn't just the hockey tryouts; it was everything. In eighth grade, I kind of had life figured out and had my place. But at this new school, I didn't know what would go on and where I'd fit in. I just had to make that hockey team. Had to run that seven-minute mile. Had to!

-2-

I love these night games. So many people can fill the stands and cheer you on. The score is still tied. Out of the corner of my eye, I see the timer moving toward the ref — seconds left now. I feel the tension in the air creeping over my skin. My fullback sends me a crisp hard hit, and I glide into the pass moving like lightning and catch it on my stick. The crowd is roaring. It's all up to me now. I hear pounding footsteps behind me. Have to hurry. I bring my stick back to shoot. The goalie's going down and....

"Get moving, Jackie." It was my mom's voice. *What? Was she cheering too?* "We'll be late for the hairdresser."

I was dreaming. I wanted to ignore her. Keeping my eyes closed, I tried to stay in my dream, but it was already starting to fade away. *Come on, come on. Let me get to that spot.*

"Jackie, now!"

"Okay, okay!" I was awake.

I rolled out of bed but sat on the edge for just a minute, kind of gathering my thoughts. I **so** wanted to score in that

8

dream. Would that be cool or what? I'd actually had a couple of dreams like that this summer. One thing puzzled me, though. Just as I was getting ready to shoot, I would wake up or the dream would change all of a sudden and I would never know if I scored. Actually, it was starting to get annoying. I really wanted to get to the end of the dream and see myself make the shot. I wondered if it meant something, that I could never see myself score.

Later that morning, driving along with my mom, my mind began re-spinning my thoughts about high school. Northfield was enormous. Getting lost could be so easy. It would be mortifying to walk into a class late with everyone staring at you and thinking you were some dumb freshman just because you couldn't find the right room. High school would be so much better if I could just show up at the hockey field in the afternoon and not worry about the rest of the day.

Mom interrupted my worries. "Jackie, now that you are entering high school, how about trying something new and different with your hair? You have been wearing that same old ponytail since third grade. Isn't it time for something a little more grown up?" I started to feel the hairs on the back of my neck stand up. *Danger, danger!*

See, my mom has a way of sneaking around a person and attacking things indirectly when she wants something, so I was feeling a little uneasy about the hair comment. Sometimes I thought she would make a real good stalker; you wouldn't know she was even there and all of a sudden she would pounce, having you where she wanted you.

I tried to put some heat into my reply, as if to say *I know your game*, when I said, "My ponytail is just fine. It's easy to put up and keep out of my eyes when I play."

"Well," she said, throwing some attitude right back, "you don't play sports all day."

I would if I could, I thought. But I didn't say this out loud since I knew it would only start another heated argument about my interest in sports. She just didn't get it, and my dad stayed out of it. I knew Matt would understand my feelings because he loved playing soccer. I couldn't understand why my mom wasn't all over him about how he looked but could still find time to bug me. It wasn't fair.

We finally pulled Sherman's Tank — that's what we called our family's old SUV — into a parking space close to the sign that read "Serendipity Spa." Getting out of the car, I took a second look at the sign. *What a dumb name!* I didn't even know what the word serendipity meant. When you walk into a place, you should know what it's all about, right? Like when you see a sign for "Tony's Pizza," you know a guy named Tony is going to sell you a slice of pie.

We waited at the reception desk for Mr. Johns, the salon owner. The place was buzzing, and I wrinkled my nose at the mixture of smells of hairspray, nail polish remover, and other things I couldn't even identify. Mom started to thumb through a magazine, and my eyes kind of glazed over at the entire scene.

Then I zeroed in on something familiar. Two girls from my class, Emma Connors and Ashley Walsh, who thought they were all that, were sitting next to each other getting their toes polished. In eighth grade, they had been all into the boy drama. When they got the boys' attention, it was like they were earning a Girl Scout merit badge or something. My friends and I mostly stayed away from them.

Anyway, they spotted me at the same time. I would have liked to have pretended I didn't see them, but I heard their high pitched voices call out.

"Oh, Jackie, you're getting a pedicure too? How fun," they squealed with fake interest, not giving me enough time to answer. I happen to know that if it wasn't for my brother, they wouldn't even have spoken to me.

Then Emma went on. "So how is your brother?" Not taking a breath, Emma turned to Ashley. "He's *so* cute!"

"Everyone we know loves him," Ashley said.

Emma broke in, "Is he still going with that girl from East Morris High School?"

"No, fine, yes," I said quickly, answering their rapid fire questions. I wished I didn't have to say anything at all, but Mom would have jumped on me for being rude, so I was stuck.

I was saved from making any further comment by Mr. Johns taking me by the arm as he fussed over my mom, saying, "My dear, it has been ages, yet your cut still looks beautiful. How do you manage to look younger every time I see you?" His mouth ran on nonstop as he led me to his shampoo chair all the way at the back of the salon.

After the wash job, I was seated in Mr. Johns' number one station and had the time to take a long look at myself in the mirror. Normally I was a pretty cheerful person, but staring back at me was one very gloomy face. *What am I doing here?*

As I looked at my reflection more closely, I tried to imagine what other people saw. I have a heart-shaped face; at least, that's what the twins and I decided last year when we were looking through one of their mother's fashion magazines. Maybe they would notice my light green eyes. If I had a good feature at all, I thought it was that one. My eyes were an unusual shade, which was kind of cool, and I have to be honest — I lucked out in the eyelashes department 'cause they were thick and long.

But my skin was so pale, and I had freckles that never went away across the bridge of my nose. I'd much rather be dark like the twins. But I guess it was an okay face; I mean, no one ever called me names over it. And it's not like a face was going to get anyone closer to a sub-seven-minute mile, right?

Mr. Johns came over to my chair and had my mom sit in the empty chair next to me. I could tell they'd been talking, and I didn't like it one little bit. I was getting that trapped feeling.

"Oh my," said Mr. Johns, "so much hair for this delicate face. It simply overpowers her." *Is he really not talking to me? Hello, it's my head.* He went on speaking to my mom like I wasn't there. "I think under those long dark tresses there is a little Audrey Hepburn in there somewhere."

Who's Audrey Hepburn? I wondered. *Something tells me she's probably not an athlete.*

Mom swiveled in her chair and faced me. "Honey, it would make me so happy if you started school with a little more polish." Before I could say boo, Mom went on. "How about you let Mr. Johns cut your hair, and then I'll take you to Sports Authority and treat you to those new warm ups you've been wanting?"

Mom, how can you stoop so low as to bribe your own daughter? But I really, really want those sweats. They're even Northfield navy blue. What's a little inch I guess?

"Okay, but not too short, okay?"

Mom smiled. She knew she'd won this round. "Don't worry. Mr. Johns knows what he is doing."

With that, Mr. Johns spun the chair around and started snipping away. For twenty minutes, I sat there with Mr. Johns' constant chatter mixing in with my falling curls, his fingers running through my hair depositing gooey gel, and then the fluffy blow drying. The whole thing was making me nervous. He finally whisked me around to face the mirror. "Ta da!" he proudly said, bringing his hands up in the air like a magician at the end of some crazy trick.

"Oh, Jackie," said Mom, "you look beautiful!" I couldn't believe my mom said that.

*Beautiful? You've got to be kidding! Who **am** I? There's some stranger in the mirror.* All I could see was this mess of curls no longer than my chin and NO PONYTAIL! My eyes started to fill up. *Why did I let this happen? How can I start school looking like this, and what about my hair for hockey?*

I bolted out of the chair and ran to the car before anyone could see my tears. That would have been the clincher. I waited by the car and my mom eventually came out after paying the bill. "Jackie," she said in her calm, everything will be all right voice, "you are just not used to it. It will be okay." She slipped into the driver's seat and paused a moment. "You really look adorable, you know."

"Are you serious? I look horrible. I just want to go home." I turned away and stared out the window, but everything was looking a little blurry. Mom started the car and asked if I wanted to get the sweat suit, but I snapped, "No way." As I continued to gaze at people walking by on the sidewalk, I wondered if any of them ever started school with crappy hair.

Mom put the car in gear and didn't say another word, but I thought of one — betrayer! When we arrived home, I jumped out of the car and slammed the door, raced up the front steps, and went straight to my room.

After a lot of crying, I must have fallen asleep 'cause the next thing I knew, my dad was rubbing my shoulder.

"Jackie, talk to me."

I kept my head buried under the pillow. I didn't want him to see me, and I clutched my special 'comforter,' Bubby, a one-eared rabbit, closer to me.

"Mom is so sorry you are upset. She just wanted the best for you. Turn around."

"No," I said, my voice kind of muffled in the pillow. "I look ugly."

"Jackie, you could never look ugly to me." I could hear that he meant it, but a dad would always say that stuff. His voice became more firm. I could tell he was not going to let me have my sulk any longer.

"You would be beautiful even if you were completely bald. Come on, where is that McKendry spirit? Hey, didn't some rock star shave her head? She still had everyone following her around."

He was trying. I had to give him that. In a few moments, I turned around on the bed.

"Oh, Dad, it's awful," I cried as I reached out to him.

Dad gave me a long hug and said, "All right, stand up and let me have a look at you." For a few moments he just stared. "Jackie," he said, "I'll be honest with you. I don't see my little girl anymore."

"Dad," I cried.

"Let me finish, Jackie. What I see is a young woman, or at least the young woman you will become someday. I just didn't think I would see her so soon. You know, if you don't want to keep your hair this way, it'll grow and you can have your ponytail back, right?"

"I guess," I said with a sniff.

"Let's go downstairs and see your mother. She feels really bad."

Mom was standing at the kitchen sink when I came in. She turned when she heard my footsteps. "I am so sorry, Jackie," she said. "I was wrong; I should have never pressured you to cut your hair. No more Mr. Johns, unless you ask for him."

I was torn. I was still angry with her, but I knew her apology was for real. I felt my body cave and sighed.

"Okay, Mom," I said, but I was thinking, *Don't worry, that won't happen anytime soon.*

I walked over and gave her a hug 'cause she wanted one. She thought it was all okay, but it wasn't, not for me. When school started, I'd probably have to bring an identity card because no one would believe I was the Jackie McKendry they knew; they would think I was just some fake who was

15

trying to pass herself off as an athlete, but really wasn't one. After school, they'd probably send me to the band room or Spanish club. I could feel the tears start to come and hurried from the room.

I stayed in bed pretty late the next morning. Losing so much hair seemed to have taken away all my energy, but eventually I knew my day needed starting because my stomach was giving me the heads up that it wanted food. I walked into the bathroom, hoping my hair didn't look as bad as I remembered. Maybe it had grown six inches overnight. I stared in the vanity mirror and a stranger looked back at me. It was way worse; it was a total disaster. Tears came to my eyes. "Mom!"

Coming down the hall, she must have heard my shriek. How could she not?

"Look, it's a mess. This is all your fault!"

Mom sighed and tried to calm me down. "Jackie, remember what Mr. Johns said? Just put a little gel on your fingertips and run your fingers through your hair; then squeeze the waves the way you want them to shape to your head. Here, let me show you."

After she finished, she made me look in the mirror. "Jackie, you really needed to stop looking like a little girl."

She squeezed my shoulder and added, "You're in high school now."

I stared back at myself, thinking, *Maybe I liked being the way I was. Did you ever think of that?* I had to admit she did make it look a little better, but could I really do it myself, and at 6:15 tomorrow morning? I wasn't so sure on that one.

"Jackie, come downstairs and have an early lunch. Then you can help me with some work in the yard before you meet up with the twins."

The thought of leftover lasagna finally brought a little happiness to my morning. After helping my mom with the yard work, I grabbed a bottle of water from the fridge and gathered up my hockey stuff. I stopped for a moment and debated what to do with my hateful hair. Running upstairs, I grabbed a bandana that I sometimes used as a sweat rag, folded it in a triangle, and tied it in the back. Only then did I head off for the park.

The bike ride definitely helped me let off steam. I finally started to feel a little like the old me again and decided that practicing hockey one more time would also help chase away my blues.

The twins were putting their bikes in the bike rack when I got to the park. "What's with the scarf?" Jules asked.

It was now or never. If I couldn't share bad stuff with my best friends, my parents might as well ship me off to Siberia to work in the salt mines or something. I untied the knot.

"Wow," said Jules. "Turn around."

Tori stared at me for a bit longer before saying, "It's so different…but it looks great."

I could feel my eyes getting all teary again. "Don't be nice. My mom made me — well, almost made me. I feel awful. I'm just not me anymore."

"Maybe it's time for a new you," Jules said.

"What's the matter with the old me?"

"Nothing," Jules said. "I didn't mean it like that. I just think that going to a new school gives everyone a chance to kind of experiment, try things out."

"But what will I do with it at hockey practice with it so short? There is no way I can get my hair into a ponytail." Tori walked around me, checking my new look out, and then came to my rescue by saying she'd look through magazines and figure something out.

Jules interrupted us. "Okay, enough talk about hair. Look, they just cut the grass so conditions are great for practicing. Let's jog down to the end of the field and back, and then we can start hitting."

Soon all we heard were the familiar sounds of balls being stopped and hit.

"Keep your stick on the ground!"

"Move your feet!"

"Look up before you hit!"

We called back and forth. Because the three of us had played together for so long, we could say this stuff to each other without anyone throwing a hissy fit. After about an hour, we were finished and started walking back to our bikes.

Packing her hockey stuff on her bike, Tori turned and asked what I was going to wear to school the next day. I knew this was supposed to be a big deal, like first impressions could label you for the next four years of your life or something. But I just shrugged my shoulders and said I wasn't sure. To pacify her, I told her I was planning on wearing my navy shorts and my brother's old soccer shirt for practice, hoping that would make her think I was on it.

Couldn't fool old Tori; she gave me a look as if to say, knock, knock, is anybody home? But she went on. "Jules and I are wearing new crop pants our Nana gave to each of us for our birthday. We haven't even worn them yet because we were saving them for school."

"What color?" I asked, trying to throw some interest her way.

"Black," Jules said, "but we are wearing different shirts, and since Tori is wearing her hair down, I'll wear mine up in a ponytail."

At the mention of the word ponytail, I froze and swallowed hard. From the look on Jules' face, I could tell she was sorry she said the word.

"Its okay, Jules, you can say it. I'll live," I said, hoping I was right.

"Hey, we'll look for you in the auditorium," Tori said as she mounted her bike. "You coming, Jules?"

"In a minute."

"It'll be a mob scene," Tori called over her shoulder as she started off down the bike path. "If I miss you, good luck, Jackie."

Jules waited a moment and then turned to me. "You going to be okay?"

"Yeah, I guess." I retied my bandana, but Jules walked over and pulled it off.

"You really don't need this. Personally," she said as she studied me again, "I think it makes you stand out." She stuck the bandana in her back pocket.

I smiled at my friend. She meant well, but the thing of it was, I wanted to look just like everyone else, ponytail and all. I hopped on my bike and took off in the opposite direction, still stressing about my hair.

At 8:30 that night, Jules called. "Hey, Jackie, you all set for school tomorrow?"

"I guess, Jules. I'm as ready as I'm ever going to be."

"Missing anything?" Jules laughed.

"What? What arc you talking about, Jules?"

"Your hockey stick. You left it at the park. Were you planning on dribbling the ball down the field with your feet tomorrow, Jackie? The ball is pretty hard, you know."

How could I have forgotten something as important as my stick? I felt like dying. *What if Jules hadn't seen it and someone just picked it up and threw it away?* "I can't believe I did that," I finally said.

"Don't worry, Jackie, I've got it. I'll bring it tomorrow and give it to you at practice."

"Jeez, thanks, Jules. I'm such an airhead. What would I do without you?"

"Have sore feet, I guess. See you tomorrow, Jackie."

I lay back on the bed, thinking about school. I could just picture it. Hi, Ms. O'Donnell, my name is Jacqueline McKendry, but you can call me Jackie. Oh, where's my stick? Well, I used to have a stick, but I left it in the park. Can I be a part of the team? I could just see her mentally looking down the list and putting a big 'L' for loser by my name.

I must have said something out loud 'cause Lizzie called from the other twin bed, "Jackie, did you say something?"

"No, Lizzie, go back to sleep." I turned over onto my stomach, grabbed my pillow and put it over my head. Starting tomorrow, I might have to start making lots of reminder lists, and I wished with all my heart that it was going to be the hardest thing about my first day of high school.

-4-

The alarm sounded and I groaned. *Six o'clock, it's barely light out.* My sister, who didn't start school yet, buried her head under her covers. "Sorry, Lizzie," I whispered, tiptoeing into the bathroom. I could tell from the steam on the mirror that Matt had already been up and gone. I took a quick shower and then put the gel in my hair. The haircut did look better, I guessed, so maybe I had progressed from 'totally ugly' to 'not worth mentioning.' When I thought of the day in front of me, maybe having boring hair would be the least of my problems. I could live with boring right then. In the back of my mind, though, I thought I should at least see if the drugstore had anything that would grow hair fast.

I slipped on my jeans, sneakers, and a short-sleeved pink hoodie, which was stashed in the back of my closet, and I took the necklace that Matt had given me for Christmas last year out of my jewelry box. It was a silver chain with the number ten charm, my old hockey uniform number. Maybe I'd get lucky number ten again this year. I hoped so.

Finally I put in my silver studs, and then I remembered — sports watch; okay, ready! I reached under my desk for my backpack that held my hockey gear and quietly slipped down the stairs.

In the kitchen, Mom was already up. "Good morning, Jackie, feeling excited for your first day? What would you like for breakfast?"

I told her I didn't know 'cause my stomach was starting to bubble up with nerves and I wasn't sure I could keep anything down. Trying to think of something else besides food, I asked, "Where's Matt?"

"He left twenty minutes ago. He's picking up the girlfriend and taking her to school at East Morris." I've noticed that Mom often referred to Matt's girl, Cheri, as 'the girlfriend.' I wasn't sure she really cared for Cheri that much.

"Your father and I are concerned about all the morning traffic and Matt having to get up a half hour earlier, so we'll see how it works out. To tell you the truth, I'm not so sure this riding to school together thing wasn't Cheri's idea. Your brother is always trying to please her."

She put some toast and juice in front of me, insisting that I needed something in my stomach. I looked at what she brought me. I swear the toast tasted like cardboard, and I didn't take more than a few bites. For once, my stomach couldn't handle any more food.

At the bus stop, three other freshmen who lived in my neighborhood were waiting. This was the first time they were taking a school bus, too. Thank goodness there were no upperclassmen at our stop 'cause I had heard they could really bust on freshmen. I went over and said hi. They seemed hardly aware of me standing there; they probably thought I was a transfer or something since I didn't have my trademark ponytail.

I couldn't stand the silence anymore; everyone seemed so edgy. I just blurted out, "I'm so nervous I think I'm going to barf."

That seemed to break the tension, and I guess they recognized me because they all kind of smiled and said they felt the same. One of the girls said, "I can't wait to get our schedules!"

"When do we get them?" I asked.

"I think we get them in homeroom," the boy said. "My sister told me that when we go to the auditorium, they'll call out our names and give us our homeroom number."

When the bus arrived, we all climbed in, and at the next stop, some upperclassmen did get on. Somehow we stayed calm, at least on the outside, and tried to look cool around the older kids, like we did this all the time. On the inside, I think we were super anxious 'cause we all had to know deep down that we were all starting a brand new life.

When we arrived at school, everyone piled out of the bus like they knew where they were going. I had no clue. I decided that the other freshmen must know where the auditorium was, so I followed them.

The room was packed and noisy. There were so many people moving about, talking and shouting. I looked around for the twins and for a place to sit with friends, but I soon gave up on finding anyone and quickly plopped down in the first empty seat I could find.

At eight o'clock, an old guy moved to the center of the stage, took the microphone, and asked for everyone's attention. When the room got quiet, he introduced himself as Dr. Bartlett, the principal, and welcomed everyone to the school. Then he started calling out names and homerooms.

"Julianna Hanson, A 105; Victoria Hanson, C 213."

I sat up in my seat. I looked around and saw the twins slowly exiting toward the rear of the auditorium. Jules was walking in her usual straight-ahead, no-nonsense way, but for Tori it was more of a stop and go. She seemed to be checking out the other students. I smiled to myself, imagining she was scanning the room for new boyfriend material on the very first day of school. Tori definitely had her priorities.

When they reached the back of the room, they seemed to hesitate for a moment; then they turned and went in different directions. It seemed strange not to see them together. It was like they were chopped in two, and it made me wonder why it was happening.

The guy on stage was still reading names so I stopped thinking about the twins and tried to concentrate on the principal's list. Since I missed freshman orientation this summer because I was visiting Grandma McKendry, I was feeling a little lost and I was no closer to solving the mystery of what the letters meant in front of the room numbers.

My nerves started to spike again, and I hoped I remembered deodorant this morning. I knew I couldn't fake my cluelessness anymore. Something had to happen. I turned to the boy seated next to me and asked, "What do the letters mean in front of the room numbers?"

The boy stared at me for the longest moment. *Jeez...he thinks I'm an idiot.* Then he told me that A wing held the math and computer science rooms, while B wing had English and social studies on the first floor and foreign languages and business on the second floor. Then there was C wing, which was for the science department and industrial arts.

"Look," he said, "when your name is called, if you have A, go out those doors," he pointed to the doors in the back of the auditorium, "and turn left. If you have C, turn right. If you have B, go out the front of the room, and B wing is straight ahead."

I nodded my head. "Got it."

"Mitchell Kennedy," the principal's voice boomed out. The boy next to me started to move around in his seat, but he didn't get up. More names were called, and then I heard, "Jacqueline McKendry, B 132." I popped up and moved toward the front of the auditorium.

I didn't get farther than a couple of rows when I heard, "Hey, Reds, wait up. Reds, I'm talking to you in the pink shirt!"

I turned. It was the same boy who had given me the directions. I frowned 'cause I've always hated being called Reds. He must have noticed the expression on my face since he said, "Hey, I didn't mean anything. Come on, I'm going to the same homeroom as you. Hi," he said as he walked toward me, extending his hand. "My name is Mitch, Mitch Kennedy."

I hesitated, and instead of reaching out and taking his hand I moved my hand away from his and nervously touched my hair. I was still worked up about how it looked and felt totally awkward. Standing there, I looked up and noticed how tall he was with really broad shoulders. His size was a little intimidating. It made me feel little and too young, as if I really belonged back in elementary school.

Finally I said, "Nobody has ever called me Reds."

"Oh really? They definitely should," he said, smiling.

His smile, it made me nervous. But I thanked him just the same and said that I could get there on my own. I turned on my heels and marched down the aisle. I barely heard the long, slow whistle from behind me. I just ignored it and kept walking right out the auditorium door.

The hallways were crowded with people moving in a dozen different directions. It looked like they all knew where they were going but me. My eyes darted around, trying to find spaces that I could sneak through like I did on the hockey field. *Maybe if I hired a couple of bodyguards like those Hollywood stars have, I could fight through this mess a lot more easily. I can just picture it — two big, burly dudes saying 'make way, make way.' Yeah, I should definitely recommend that to all the graduating eighth graders next year.*

It seemed like hours, but it was only ten minutes later when I finally found room B 132. Fortunately, there were others who had trouble finding the room too, so I slipped in unnoticed, quickly saw an empty seat toward the back and headed that way. That was when I spotted the tall boy from the auditorium giving me a little smile. *Great, I haven't been in this school for an hour and already somebody knows what a numbskull I am.*

The teacher got up to speak, but my mind was still back in the auditorium with the boy. *Why was I so uptight? He must think I'm such a dork. He was just being helpful.*

Sometimes I just didn't get why I couldn't act more like a normal human being.

"Attention, people," the teacher in the front of the class finally said. "My name is Mr. Jackson, and fortunately for all of you, I will not be your teacher unless you are taking senior English. In a few moments, when your name is called, come up and get your class schedule."

While I was waiting my turn, I looked around the room and saw two of my teammates from eighth grade hockey, Ellen Burns and Lindsay Sayers, sitting by the windows. I smiled at them and mouthed "Hi," and they waved back. The room seemed a little friendlier to me now that I found some familiar faces.

My name was called, and back in my seat I began studying my schedule. Okay, first period, Spanish I; second, English; and third, study hall or physical education, depending on the day of the week. I had lunch next followed by Algebra I, Earth Science, and finally World History. It looked like a long day to me and a lot of homework to get done after dinner 'cause I planned to be doing something else to fill my afternoons. But at least I could get English done in study hall on two days, and that'd be good.

The most important thing was not even written on my schedule, but it was going to be the best part of the day. I knew it by heart: three o'clock hockey practice. I looked over at Ellen and Lindsay and made an eating motion with my hands then drew a question mark in the air. Ellen shot back five fingers and I made a thumbs down sign. Lindsay held up four fingers and I smiled with a thumbs up. At least I'd know one person at lunch.

Mr. Jackson assigned us our hall lockers and said we had ten minutes to go to our lockers and make sure we could do our combinations. I grabbed Lindsay as we went out the door. "Linds, if you see any of the gang, find out what lunch they have. Maybe we can get a table."

"Okay, Jackie," Lindsay said, then looked at me a second time. "Your hair looks flaming hot, but weren't you nervous getting it cut so short? I would die if I didn't have my ponytail." I smiled and shrugged my shoulders, trying hard not to have a boohoo moment. I really needed to toughen up about my stupid hair.

Following the opening and closing of lockers and the memorization of combinations, Mr. Jackson went through the Northfield list of school rules and regulations step by boring step. It was definitely a big yawn, and I started to tune him out. I looked at my watch. It was still only 9:20. *Jeez, this day is going to last forever.*

Finally, Mr. Jackson announced that when the bell rang, we would be going through an abbreviated schedule for the day. I glanced at the map and then my class schedule one last time. *Spanish in room B 218. You can do this, Jackie.* My fingers were crossed as the bell rang. My first two classes were a blur; luckily, they were easy to find. Next was physical education. The day was beginning to look up.

Not! When I got to the gym, there were a ton of boys and girls in there. At first it seemed as confusing as the auditorium. Some big guy divided us up, and it turned out that there were four different classes in the gym at the same time. It was so different from my old school. Couldn't anything be like eighth grade?

My gym teacher turned out to be the varsity hockey coach, Mrs. Fortunato. That made me doubly nervous, but excited too. As I sat in the bleachers waiting for her to go through our class list, I kind of checked her out. She was small and trim with short salt and pepper hair, maybe my mom's age. She looked way different than my coach in elementary school, Ms. Nelson, who was very nice, but she had to have been at least eighty and she didn't always remember who played where on the field.

Something told me that this would never happen with this lady. In fact, rumors were that she was a real disciplinarian and very demanding. Since she'd won three state championships, my guess was that she must be a really great coach, so I knew I needed to do a good job in this class.

When she came to my name, she looked up and asked if I was related to Matt McKendry. I was kind of used to that question since everyone knew my brother and what a good athlete he was. When I said that I was his sister, she asked me if I played soccer like Matt did.

"No, field hockey," I said.

"Oh, I'm always happy to hear that answer. I look forward to seeing you play sometime. Next, Ben Pardo..." and on the coach went. For some reason, I decided I might be lucky to be in her class.

By lunch, I was starving. Going through the lunch line, I thought that I definitely needed to eat a better breakfast or stash a couple of energy bars in my backpack.

Two kids were behind me, pushing and shoving each other, and one of them said to me with a smirk on his face, "Hey Annie, where's your dog, Sandy?" His friend laughed and I hurried away, feeling humiliated that he thought I looked like that girl in the movie. Guys could be so mean sometimes.

I finished paying, trying to blink away some moisture that must have gotten into my eyes, when I heard someone calling my name. "Jackie, over here, over here." It was Jules, yelling and waving her arm.

It felt good to see a friend in this big cafeteria with an empty seat right beside her. I suddenly realized I'd found a safe place in all this craziness. Maybe now, I could survive the rest of the day.

Two other hockey girls, Lindsay, from homeroom, and Britt Hollaway, the manager of our eighth grade hockey team, were at the table. The fourth girl was Alisha Wahler, who was our eighth grade class vice-president.

"This is a great table, guys, just like last year," I said, sliding into the seat next to Jules. "Where's Tori?"

"Saw her in gym and checked out her schedule. She has a later lunch," Jules said.

"Don't you have any classes together?"

"No, just gym. Our parents asked the guidance department to give us separate schedules. I'm just glad we'll be together for hockey."

As we were gulping down our food, Lindsay decided to make an announcement. "Jackie's got an admirer."

"No way," said Jules, and all the eyes at the table turned to me.

"What are you talking about, Lindsay?" I said, suddenly feeling my face growing warm.

"There's this tall, good-looking dude in our homeroom. I don't know his name, but he could not take his eyes off Jackie this morning," she said.

"Don't be ridiculous," I shot back at her. "He's just some guy who gave me directions in the auditorium. It's nothing."

"We'll see," Lindsay said as she winked at Jules.

As we finished our lunch, I noticed some girls at another table whispering and pointing at our table. "Who are they?" I asked Jules. "Why are they staring at us?"

"I think they're from Morrisville Middle School. Remember when we tied them and then the game went into overtime last year?" Jules said.

"I remember," Britt whispered as she leaned across Lindsay. "I was sitting at the scorers' table last year, and their manager gave me the scoop. Morrisville had been really worried about playing us, and since their school had won the eighth grade championship for two years in a row, they didn't want to be the Morrisville team that gave up the championship trophy. Their manager said they really hated us for almost taking it away from them."

"That was a physical game," Jules said. "They knocked you on the ground a couple of times, Jackie."

I grinned. "I hope I don't have to start wearing shoulder pads and a helmet to practice." Everyone laughed at that picture because I'm such a little peanut compared to most players. Just then, the bell rang. "Guess we better get going. See you guys later."

Algebra and Earth Science were no biggie, but I did notice two of the Morrisville girls from lunch in my science class. They just stared at me. *Give it a rest.* I wondered why they couldn't forget about last year. I mean, they won it, so what was their deal?

My last class of the day was World History, and all I could think about was that in forty minutes, I'd be on the hockey field. I was so wrapped up in my thoughts about practice and doing my timed run that I didn't see where I was going, and I collided with another student as I passed through the doorway. Tumbling down to the floor, my books went scattering everywhere.

I felt two strong hands reach out and pull me up. Everyone was looking at me and I felt mortified. Before I could even think straight, I heard my rescuer laughing as he scooped up my books from the floor. *Oh no, the guy from the auditorium.*

"Reds, you have to stop resisting your attraction to me," he said, standing up.

Totally embarrassed, I finally spat out, "I am not attracted to you or anybody else," and I snatched my books from his hands. He raised an eyebrow, then let me pass. I hurried down the aisle to find an empty seat. *The nerve of that guy. What conceit! Don't tell me he's in this class.*

It turned out that Mitch Kennedy was in my class, and he took a seat right behind me. I was really hot by now. I wished he would just disappear.

The next moment, he was leaning forward and whispering, "Sorry if I made you upset just then, Jackie." His comment was such a surprise and sounded so sincere that I realized how silly I was being. *It must be my first day nerves.* I felt myself relax and my breathing slowed down.

I half turned in my seat. "It's okay."

He sat back, but not before I heard him say, kind of quiet like, "That's good."

As the teacher started talking, I watched the hands on the clock slowly move toward the last six minutes of class. I could hardly pay attention to what he was saying. I could feel the butterflies building. This was what I had been waiting for all summer, but it was also the moment I had been dreading. What if I didn't make the run?

-5-

When the bell rang, I was out the door in a flash, moving quickly toward my locker to pick up my stuff for practice.

My heart was pumping fast with excitement by the time I got to the girls' locker room. There were so many girls there. Not everyone was getting ready for freshman hockey practice, either. There were varsity hockey players, cross-country girls, and soccer players, too. I looked around to see how things worked, and saw that the girls used their gym locks and lockers for practice, too. I quickly changed into my brother's old soccer shirt, one he had worn years ago when he was a munchkin like me, and hoped it would bring me luck.

Fifteen minutes later, most of the older girls had left the locker room. Just as the rest of us were leaving, an older hockey player peeked in from the doorway and yelled to us, "Hey, freshmen, check the sign at the door. You're supposed to meet your coach on the track. Better get moving."

At the track, all the girls were checking each other out. They were trying to pretend that they weren't, but they really were. Everyone wanted to know where the competition was — and so did I.

Most of my eighth grade teammates were standing together, minus our sweeper, Abby Sanders, who had stopped playing hockey to do band. I recognized some of the Morrisville players camped out together, but there were a lot of girls who were new to me.

In about five minutes, Ms. O'Donnell, the coach, arrived, which was a good thing 'cause I was just about bouncing out of my skin by then. She stood in front of us with her clipboard, not saying anything in her white three-buttoned shirt and navy shorts, complete with a whistle on a lanyard around her neck. It seemed to me like she was waiting, maybe for us to shut up and give her our attention. She looked really young with her blond ponytail, almost like one of us. *Boy, I wish I could tan like that. She looks so fit. I bet she could really play hockey.*

Finally it was quiet and the coach started to speak. "My name is Ms. O'Donnell, and I'd like to welcome you to Northfield. This is my first day, too, and I hope you're as excited to be here as I am. I want you to know I have very high hopes for this team. As many of you know, Northfield has a reputation for having an exceptional hockey program. This didn't happen by accident, but because a lot of girls wanted the program to be great. They all worked hard, and the very best of them always put the team first. This is the most important thing you're going to learn this year. Remember, each of us affects all of us, and what happens to one happens to all."

I was getting pumped. I really liked what she was saying. I turned to Tori and Jules and saw that they were excited too. Looking around at the others, I saw some players looking kind of puzzled. Maybe not everyone got it. How couldn't they? It seemed to me that this coach knew what being on a team was all about.

After the warm up, she divided us into groups and had each group line up on the start line. We were supposed to run around the track four times to make a mile. When we crossed the finish line, she would call out our times.

I was in the second group with Tori and Lindsay. When it was our turn to run, I could feel the butterflies in my stomach. As we lined up, I was really glad that Tori and Lindsay were right next to me. Tori whispered, "All right, it's us, one, two, three," and she gave my arm a squeeze. By the second lap, half of the group was still close together, but some girls were dropping back and a few started jogging.

At the end of the third lap, Ms. O'Donnell called out our time as we ran by. Mine was 5:04.

Hearing the time, I was feeling good and my confidence started to grow. This was no Browman's Hill, just a flat surface.

I called over to Tori, "Let's go."

At 5'9", Tori was all legs and could really cover distance with her long strides. While I was barely 5'2", I was pretty quick, and soon the last lap became a two-girl race. As we crossed the finish line, Ms. O'Donnell called out 6:35 for me and 6:46 for Tori.

"Good job," Jules called as she jogged over to us and gave us a high five. I was so relieved it was over. Jules' group was last, and it included Becky Weiss, our eighth grade goalkeeper, Ellen, and the two K's, or the K-K's as everyone called Kate Ross and Katie Hart.

With most of the runs done, most of us were feeling loose and relaxed. A lot of us started cheering for the last group, wanting them to do well. Finally, there was some good excitement in the air and not just everyone's bad nerves. The best time so far had been my 6:35, and Ms. O'Donnell challenged these last runners to beat it. "Go," she called, and they took off.

Everyone was cheering and calling out names. The Morrisville girls, obviously, were cheering for their three players. Athletes from the third public school, Gibbstown, were urging their lone player on, and the players from my school were loudest of all. I was sure who would come in first, though. It was Becky, the goalie, the quickest athlete from our school. I couldn't imagine anyone faster than her.

As the group entered the final turn, one of the girls bumped into Becky and Becky went down. The girl, someone I didn't know, went flying by at the finish line with her arms in the air in triumph — "6:34." Meanwhile, Jules, who was just a short distance behind them, stopped running and bent down to help Becky. Tori and I ran over to help.

"Are you okay?" Tori asked.

I think I sprained my ankle," Becky said. We could hear the pain in her voice.

Ms. O'Donnell came up behind us. "Girls, let's help Becky up and get her over to the bench. I'll call for the trainer."

The trainer took charge of Becky, and Ms. O'Donnell moved the rest of us away and told us to jog down to the freshmen field to start the rest of practice. I was surprised; Ms. O'Donnell demonstrated each skill she wanted us to do. I mean, she could really do the stuff. We started with the dribble, and soon I was going in and out of cones, trying to keep the ball right on my stick like Ms. O'Donnell showed us. It wasn't as easy as she made it seem. The ball kept bouncing away from my stick every time I touched it, and I started to feel frustrated with myself. When I looked around, though, I saw that everyone else was pretty much in the same boat.

Ms. O'Donnell called us in. "I know it's a challenge to keep the ball and stick connected, but it's an important skill to have. Once you can do it, it will be hard for an opponent to take the ball from you. It takes lots of practice; you have to be patient. Next we're going to review push passing and receiving the ball." My first high school practice was underway.

At 5:30, Ms. O'Donnell brought us all in together. "Girls, you've worked hard today, and I think that's terrific. Tomorrow we will start moving the ball down the field as a team. Then we'll focus on shooting from the edge of the striking circle." Everyone got excited with that one 'cause everyone liked to shoot.

She reminded us that there were thirty-nine girls still trying out and that she was only going to be able to keep twenty-five. She told us she would put up a list of players who made the team the following Wednesday. That was supposed to give each of us plenty of time to show her what kind of players we were.

"If you did not get under eight minutes on your run today," she said, "you will meet me at the track for one more opportunity at three o'clock tomorrow. The rest of you will meet me on the field at 3:15."

Walking back to the locker room, I thought about Jules having to do the run tomorrow 'cause she stopped to help Becky. A bunch of others girls would have to do their run again, too. For once, the idea of all those runs up Browman's Hill this summer seemed to have been a pretty smart move. But cuts were coming — ugh!

Just before I got into bed, the phone rang. "Jackie, it's for you," Mom called up. "Don't be long. Remember, it's a school night."

"Jackie, it's Jules, I didn't have a chance to ask you at practice. How was your day?"

"Okay, I guess. My teachers seem nice. How about you?"

"Not bad. It seemed a little strange not being with Tori."

"How come your parents didn't want you two together?"

"They said we depend on each other too much, but I'm not sure we do." Changing the subject, Jules asked, "What do you think of O'Donnell?"

"I like her. I think she knows her stuff so maybe we can have a really good team."

"I hope so. Some of the girls don't seem all that friendly."

"Could be they were nervous," I said.

"Maybe," said Jules. But her voice sounded as doubtful as my thinking.

Crawling into bed, I thought about how worried I had been about this first day, and now it was over. I survived and I passed the run, which was a great relief, but like Jules, I really wasn't getting very good vibes from some of the other girls who were trying out. I wondered for the first time if being on a high school team was everything it was cracked up to be.

The next day at lunch, we all started talking about practice.

"I'm a little sore today."

"Me two!"

"Me three!"

We groaned and laughed at the same time, and we called our condition 'team pain.'

"How's Becky?" Jules asked. "Has anyone seen her today? I left her a message last night but she didn't call back."

"I saw her dad driving her in when I got off the bus," Britt said. "She was on crutches."

I looked at Britt. "That stinks. We really need her. She's such a great goalkeeper." Everyone at the table agreed.

Then I got to thinking that I would be in a deep depression if that had happened to me. It was bad enough starting school, but to have to gimp around on crutches missing hockey would have been the pits. *Might as well crawl under the covers on that one,* I thought.

Jules asked Britt, "We missed you at practice yesterday. Aren't you going to be our manager this year?"

"I thought I was, but yesterday, Mrs. Fortunato asked me to be with the varsity team. I think one of their managers quit to go work after school."

"That's mad crazy, Britt, being with the varsity and all," Lindsay said, suddenly interested in the conversation.

"It's okay," Britt said. "They seem a little stuck on themselves, though." Then she smiled. "Don't worry. I'll give you guys all the dirt." We all laughed. Britt is our girl for sure.

Just then, one of the Morrisville players, a girl in navy sweats, wandered over to our table. At first I didn't recognize her, and then I noticed how her hair was pulled back low on the back of her head and wrapped with a simple rubber band. It suddenly dawned on me that she was the girl who knocked Becky down.

"So I guess all you slowpokes will be running after school," the girl grinned. I could tell she was enjoying this.

Jules spoke up. "I'm the only one. Care to join me?"

"No way," the girl said. I caught the other Morrisville girls watching all of this with interest. The girl sashayed away from us, then turned and looked over her shoulder and said, "Have fun."

"Bitch," Lindsay hissed, staring at the girl's back. I turned to her, surprised. "She bumped Becky on purpose!" Lindsay said, glaring at the girl.

"Why would she do that?" I asked.

"Because she wanted to win, no matter what," Lindsay answered as she continued to stare at the table where the girl was sitting.

"Well, you know what they say, Lindsay. What goes around, comes around," said Alisha, speaking for the first time.

I looked at Alisha. She pretty much amazed me. Even though she didn't play sports, she was definitely in tune with what went on at our table. It was like she really got the competitive thing and knew what was fair. Maybe being a class leader was like being an athlete in some ways. You know, having that 'going for it' attitude. All I knew for sure was that she was really down to earth, not some stuck-up snob like some people I'd known at my old school.

After lunch, I was getting more comfortable moving around the school and I arrived at my world history class a little early. The Mitch Kennedy guy came into the classroom right after me and once again plopped down in the seat behind me.

"How's it going, Jackie?" he said all casual like. *Relax, I said to myself, he's only some boy.*

I turned to face him and smiled. "Better than yesterday." *There, I spoke like a normal person.* "How's your day been going?" As I half listened to his reply I was thinking, *His eyes, at first I thought they were dark blue but they're really gray. Nice.*

"So where was the fire yesterday? You took off before the bell stopped ringing."

I finally focused on the conversation and said, "Field hockey practice, first day. I was kind of nervous."

"I get it; I'd feel the same way. Maybe I can see one of your games sometime."

"I have to make the team first."

"Well, good —"

Out of the blue, Mr. Coles, our history teacher, cut in. "Mr. Kennedy and Ms. McKendry, do you think you can join the rest of the class or shall we all wait for the two of you to finish your conversation?" The whole class looked back at us and laughed. I was so embarrassed. I turned three shades of pink as I faced forward and slid low in my seat. *Jackie, that's what you get for talking to some lame guy instead of paying attention in class.*

When the bell rang, Mitch whispered, "See you." I gave him a brief smile and hurried to my locker, and immediately forgot Mitch Kennedy.

The locker room seemed less crazy this time, even with all the girls. Most of the freshman hockey players took their time getting dressed since only fourteen of us needed to run at the track today.

Changing next to Ellen, I thought about Jules as well as the other girls who had to run. "Ellen, when we finish changing, we should try to get everyone out to the track and cheer the others on their run."

"Good idea," she said. Then she yelled out in the locker room, "Hey you guys, anybody want to go to the track and cheer them on?"

Most of the Washington Elementary players were all for it as well as some of the girls from Gibbstown. Walking out to the track, we were joined by two girls from Morrisville. The two Morrisville girls didn't speak to anyone at first, they just watched, but halfway through the timed run, they started to get into the cheering thing and were as loud as anybody as the run ended.

Jules and the other runners came up to us after the run and thanked us for being there for them. Then, out of habit maybe, we all put our hands in together and yelled, "Team."

Ms. O'Donnell walked up to us with a big smile on her face. "Girls, you made me very proud right now. Good job!"

Walking toward the freshman field, one of the Morris-ville runners came up to Ellen and me and thanked us for getting people to come out to the track. She introduced herself as Anna Merlino. She told us she was so anxious yesterday that she nearly threw up, but when she heard us cheering, she stopped being nervous and got a good time.

"I'm glad you passed," I said. "I get nervous sometimes, too." The girl gave me a little smile. *She seems nice. At least one of the Morrisville girls is okay.*

At the field, there were about a dozen girls standing around, waiting for the coach. Then we saw Becky sitting on the bleachers with crutches on the seat next to her. While most of the girls were getting water, Lindsay, the twins, and I went up to Becky and asked how she was doing.

It turned out that she had to be off her ankle for two weeks, and she was supposed to get treatment with the trainer during her last period physical education class.

"Ms. O'Donnell told me not to go after school because the training room would be backed up with a lot of dumb football players." She laughed. "Okay, Coach didn't say the word dumb; that was my idea. Don't worry, guys. I'll be back."

I was relieved Becky was going to be okay, but I was glad it wasn't me. I couldn't understand how she could still be so upbeat. She was one tough cookie. There were no pity games going on with her, that was for sure. Maybe that was what made her such a good goalie.

Classes passed quickly on Monday. In the afternoon, with just one more day before cuts, Ms. O'Donnell worked on our conditioning and introduced a lot of footwork drills to the practice. It was actually a lot of fun to step through the ladders, seeing how fast we could go. As practice went on, a few girls started to struggle to keep up. I could tell they probably wouldn't make it, but almost everyone was still working hard. It was going to be tough to figure out who would make the team.

Tuesday at lunch, *The Table,* as we now called ourselves, discussed the cut list. We knew a little more about the other freshman players than we had the first day, and we agreed that some people could be eliminated pretty easily. We didn't think the girls from Sacred Heart had much of a chance to make the team since their old school didn't even have a hockey program. Then I remembered one girl who was really fast. Speed counted big time in hockey, so I thought she might make it.

We knocked out four girls from Morrisville who we could tell didn't have the heart for it and just came out to be with their friends. After this mythical cut list, *The Table* was stumped.

"I can't wait for this tryout to be over," Lindsay wailed. "I just want to see my name on that list."

"We all do," Jules said. "I think we'll all make it. We have good speed and we're doing okay in the drills. The real test will be when we finally scrimmage today. That will tell who should really be with the team."

"I'm so psyched to finally be playing," I said.

"Me too," Jules said.

I walked down the aisle in my world history class. Probably 'cause my mood was amped up, I called out, "Hey, Mitch," like we had been buds for years. I smiled, but I was still thinking about the scrimmage as I put my books on the floor and slid into my seat.

"Oh, she speaks first," he laughed. "I'm making progress!"

What's that supposed to mean? "Anyway," I said, "I'm just excited because we're finally scrimmaging in practice today. We've been doing drills the whole time, which is okay, but playing is the best."

As I was babbling on, I watched his face. He seemed pretty interested in what I was saying. Then, all of a sudden, he put on a serious face, but it didn't quite get up to his eyes. He gave a little nod forward and said, "You better turn around, Ms. McKendry, or you will get yourself in trouble with Mr. Coles."

I turned forward but still had a smile on my face. *He's funny. Okay, he's also kind of cute. But what was that "progress" comment all about? Stop it, he's not important. Listen to what Mr. Coles is saying or at least think about today's scrimmage.*

Getting ready for practice, I was still thinking about Mitch Kennedy's teasing in class. He seemed nice for a boy. I just didn't know why he was wasting his time talking to me, but he did make being in class a little more interesting.

Once I got to the field I saw a million cones scattered everywhere. Ms. O'Donnell had made a series of fifteen by seven yard rectangles that looked like grids, stretched side by side, from one end of the field to the other.

"Get a partner," she called. "We're going to have a little one on one competition today. One of you will get a ball and stand at one end of the rectangle. Your partner will stand at the other end. On my whistle, the job of the attacker will be to get the ball to the other end of the grid without going out of bounds. If she can do this without fouling, she gets a point and starts again. If the defender can get the ball away from the attacker without fouling, she will get a point. Then the defender becomes the new attacker. Do you have any questions?"

"How long do we have?" someone asked.

"Thirty seconds," Ms. O'Donnell said. "Players move up a grid each time they win. The loser stays where she is. Then we start over. After twenty minutes, the player getting to the most grids is our grand winner and team champion."

Near the end of the competition, I found myself against the girl with the pale skin and mousey brown hair who had come up to our lunch table. I checked her out before the whistle blew. She looked tired, which could be a good thing for me, but her eyes were intense like she hated me or something. That was not so good.

As I studied her further, I thought that whatever this 1v1 drill was supposed to be, she was taking it as a personal challenge between us. It was just something I felt. She looked grim, like she was going to war. *Lighten up*, I wanted to yell at her.

The whistle blew. The girl started behind the line with the ball, and as I got myself in position to defend, the girl accelerated, running right at me, knocking me to the ground. The girl continued on, taking the ball over the line. It was an obvious foul on her part, but she didn't say a word to me; not sorry, have a nice day, nothing.

On the next attempt, I was alert and ready for her. As she started to speed toward me, I stepped away. It was too late for her to change direction, and when she reached the empty space I had just been in, I reached in with my stick, jabbed the ball away from her, and dribbled out the other end of the grid.

She was definitely ticked off. I mean, I could feel the steam. I started on attack, dribbling the ball into the middle of the grid. She let me pass, and then she used her stick, slamming it across my shins, causing me to trip.

"Ow, that hurts!" I said.

"Sorry," the girl replied as she picked up the loose ball and dribbled over the line.

The apology sounded fake to me. I was thinking, *Maybe Lindsay is right and this girl is just a total jerk.*

I turned to her, saying, "That's no point. You fouled me."

"Whatever," she said.

"Time," called Ms. O'Donnell, and when she asked for our scores, I quickly said "1-1" before the other girl could give her version.

"Then neither of you gets to be the winner. Too bad," Ms. O'Donnell said as she walked away. I gave the girl a look before I went to join my friends. I wished she had been the one on the bench, not Becky.

After a few more drills, Ms. O'Donnell called us all over to sit on the benches. "If I call out your name, you will go put on the red scrimmage vests and line up facing the goal nearest the school."

She started listing the names and positions. I heard my name being called for the attack line at outside left. Joining me on the team were Lindsay, Tori, Anna, and the two K's, but I didn't know the other girls. Jules, Ellen, and the fast girl from Sacred Heart were put on the other team.

We played back and forth for about ten minutes, and then the coach made substitutions. As I walked off the field, I thought I had done pretty well. At one point, I had gotten a long, cross-field feed from Anna, who had been playing right back. On Anna's pass, I had come into the striking circle out of nowhere and tipped the ball into the back of the cage. Then, before we went back to the center to restart play, I ran over to Anna, high-fived her, and let her know what a great pass she had given me. I was going to replay that goal in my head a couple of times.

As the scrimmage went on, more substitutions were made, but Jules, Lindsay, two other girls, and I never went back into the game. We kept looking at each other as we sat on the bench. I stopped playing my "golden moment" in my head and I started having doubts about where I stood with the coach.

"I feel like we're being passed over," I said to no one in particular.

Lindsay leaned over and said in a low voice so the other players couldn't hear, "Does this mean we're cut?"

"I don't know," Jules said. "She sure didn't give us much of a chance to play."

At the end of practice, Ms. O'Donnell brought us all together and thanked everyone for trying out for the team. Then she told us that there would be a list posted at 7:15 Wednesday morning on the gym bulletin board.

That night, I sat at the dining room table playing with my food. Mom said, "Jackie, with all that running you do, you must be famished. Why aren't you eating your dinner?"

"I'm just tired, Mom."

"You sure that's all, honey?" Dad asked.

Matt stopped eating long enough to add his own comment. "If you're worried about making the team, don't be. The coach would be crazy not to keep you."

That perked me up a little. "You think so, Matt?"

"Sure, you're a hard worker and you love playing. Coaches like players like that."

"But I didn't play much today. Other girls played a lot."

"Maybe she needed to watch the others more," he said. "Don't think so much, kiddo."

"Okay," I paused for a moment and then asked, "So, Mom, what do we have for desert?"

Later that night, I instant messaged the twins. They had both shared the same screen name since sixth grade; they said they did that so no one could talk behind the other sister's back.

jacmcshootr:	whats up girlie
gemsrok:	j is in bed already
	i still have more math problems 2 do
	ugh
jacmcshootr:	lol
gemsrok:	r u as nervous as i am
jacmcshootr:	yessssssss
	i want it 2 be tom already
gemsrok:	same here
	keep fingers and toes crossed
	see ya tom
jacmcshootr:	cya
gemsrok:	peace

-7-

I was standing at my corner, anxiously waiting for the bus to arrive, so keyed up that I was jiggling from one foot to another. This was it. I was either in or I was out. On the bus, I could barely sit still. My foot tapped its impatience against the seat in front of me. *Why is the driver going so slow? Hurry up already!* Finally, the bus pulled into the school drive, and little by little it moved up to its position to unload by the front door. "Easy does it," warned the bus driver as I flew out the door.

I raced down the B-wing hallway and was halted by a teacher just as I turned the corner toward the gym.

"Where are you going so fast, young lady?" the woman snapped at me. "No running in the hallways! If you don't want a detention, you better start walking."

I kept my eyes down, not looking at her, and quietly told her I would. The last thing I needed right then was trouble. Finally the teacher let me go, and feeling like I was going to explode, I speed-walked the rest of the way to the gym bulletin board.

Glancing at my watch, I saw I had just enough time to check the list and make it to homeroom. There were several girls standing in front of me talking excitedly. I couldn't see over their heads, so I had to wait for things to clear out a little and it was getting late.

I heard, "I made it, I made it," but I also noticed some girls walking away slowly, their eyes looking down at the floor. *Oh, please don't let that be me.*

I got to the front and scanned the list. Stephanie Jankowski...Anna Merlino...Jackie McKendry. *YES, I made it!* I went back over the list a second time, but more slowly. *Becky, Lindsay, Tori, Jules, Kate Ross, Ellen.* I looked one more time to see if I had missed anything. *No, I can't believe it. No Katie Hart! That stinks.* The two K's lived next door to each other and were inseparable. I wondered what Kate Ross would do without her best friend on the team. But there was no time to think about that. I had to hurry to homeroom.

I looked for Lindsay and Ellen the minute I entered the room. They were sitting in their same seats by the windows, both grinning from ear to ear. When our homeroom teacher, Mr. Jackson, came in, he looked around the room.

"Some of us look pretty happy this morning," he said. "What's going on?"

"Mr. Jackson," Lindsay said, sounding all jazzed, "Jackie, Ellen, and I all made the hockey team!"

"Congratulations, girls. Now, if you can all make the honor roll, I will really be excited."

Mitch Kennedy, who for some reason had changed his seat, was now sitting behind me in homeroom. He leaned forward. "Hey, that's great, Jackie. Congratulations!"

I looked over my shoulder, smiled automatically, and said, "Thanks." But when I turned back, I thought, *Don't pay attention to him; there are more important things to think about now.*

The bell rang and I started to pick up my books. I realized I had been in this building for almost a week, but for me, high school had started the moment I saw my name on that list. Before that moment, I had been just a visitor, some temporary tourist from the eighth grade. Now I could say I officially belonged somewhere, at least for now.

By lunchtime, we were all so pumped with the excitement of making the team that even Alisha was caught up in our celebration. "I must really be sitting at the official jock table now," she laughed.

"Well, there is that table," Jules said, pointing to the girls from Morrisville.

There were six at their table, and we were pretty sure that all six had made the team. Just then, two of the Morrisville girls got up and walked over to us. It was Anna and a girl I didn't recognize.

"Hi Jackie," Anna said to me, then looked at Jules and Lindsay. "Congratulations, you guys, on making the team."

I smiled. "You too." I turned to everyone and said, "This is Anna Merlino."

Anna introduced the new girl, Kerry Roth. "I think Becky and Kerry are going to be our team's goalies," she added.

"That's great," I said, looking at Kerry. "You're going to really like working with Becky. She's lots of fun."

"Yeah, Coach had me working with the varsity goalies for the last couple of days 'til she finished picking the team."

Britt, who had been watching all of this, suddenly got our attention when she said, "So, do you all want to know the scoop on O'Donnell?"

"Yes!" we said in unison. I wasn't usually into gossiping, but I was right on board with everyone else when it came to finding out stuff about our coach.

Jules looked at Anna and Kerry and must have seen that they wanted to be included in whatever little gems Britt was going to share with us, so she asked if they wanted to hear it too.

"Absolutely," said Anna, and Jules slid down to make room for them.

I saw Anna hesitate a moment and look over at the other table. I could see she was debating something, and then she finally sat down next to Jules. *Wow*, I thought, *Anna has thrown out the olive branch between our old schools*. I wondered if the other table thought she had crossed into enemy territory.

I caught Lindsay looking at Anna and Kerry like they were intruders or something sitting there at 'our' table, but she knew better than to say anything. She turned to Britt and said, "Spill it."

"Well, I found out stuff by talking to the other varsity manager. She has been with the team for three years so she knows everything. The old freshman coach was really lousy, the manager said, so Mrs. Fortunato used to bring up the top freshmen to play with the varsity and JV. Now that O'Donnell is here, Fortunato won't do that. That's why none of you will move up, no matter how good you are. Fortunato thinks you guys will be stronger, staying together."

"So what about O'Donnell?" Lindsay asked impatiently.

"Well, Nicky," she began, and we all smiled at Britt using the coach's nickname like they were best friends, "was supposedly a real hotshot player in high school, like all-state, and then she played at a college in Maryland and they were national champions."

"That's awesome," Anna said.

"Maybe we'll be really good then," Lindsay added. "Our eighth grade coach was okay, but I think we could have done a lot better."

"You can have a great coach and still not be a great team," Kerry said quietly.

We all just looked at her. Some of us were a little surprised, but Jules nodded her head like she agreed with what Kerry said.

Ms. O'Donnell started afternoon practice by bringing all of us together and congratulating us on making the team. She told us about her high expectations for everyone and how excited she was to be coaching us. Then she said she had something for us to start the season on the right note. She brought out a large cardboard box from behind the bleachers and set it in the middle of our circle. "I have a shirt for each of you. It is to let everyone know who we are, and it is to remind each of us of what we should be."

They were navy T-shirts with white lettering. On the front was the word "Northfield" with two crossed hockey sticks, and on the back it said "we are TEAM VIKINGS."

She told us we could pick up our shirt and our game schedule from our manager at the end of practice. Our first official game would be in two weeks.

She said, "We have a lot of work to do before our first game. From this moment on, everything we do is to get ready for that first game."

Then she did this thing with all of us that I thought was kind of cool. She had us each say our name, and we had to say one positive thing about ourselves that would contribute to the team's success. That was how I discovered two names I didn't know. Stephanie Jankowski turned out to be the speedy player from Sacred Heart, and Sam Jones was the player who knocked Becky down.

When Sam introduced herself, she said her strength was scoring, and then she gave me a smug look, daring me to say the same thing. Jules mentioned giving directions on defense. Tori grinned and said, "Keeping things fun." Somebody else talked about speed, and Anna felt the way she stayed calm in 1v1s helped the team.

Waiting for my turn, my mind was quickly flipping through possibilities, trying to figure out what to say. I wasn't going to go for "scoring goals" because Sam already said that, and I didn't really want to get into it with her. When my turn finally came, I blurted out, "Seeing open space." I don't even know where the words came from. I'm not even sure exactly what it meant, but after I said it, it just seemed right. I kind of did know where to put the ball. Sometimes, I just knew where the space was around the goalie, or who was open for a pass.

"It seems that everyone has something to give the team that is unique," Ms. O'Donnell said after we were finished.

"That is why we need every one of us in order to be a good team."

That little speech of hers gave me chills, but it didn't stop her from working us harder that practice than any other day. Becky was off her crutches but was still not back to working out, although she tried to help Kerry, who was having trouble with her clears.

Ms. O'Donnell had us come down the field in lines of three, starting at the fifty yard line. Once we got to the striking circle, whoever had the ball was to shoot. One of the other two players was to pick up the goalie rebound and then get out of the way for the next group coming down the field.

What made this drill hard was that Ms. O'Donnell was timing us from the first time we touched the ball until we got the shot off. Then she would call out our time. We were trying to beat each other's times, so we were really racing. As soon as the time was given, the next group went.

We started to get winded because the drill was going nonstop, and Ms. O'Donnell added a defender against us which made it even harder. Pretty soon, the drill fell apart. We were all getting tired and acting stupid. After five minutes of this, Ms. O'Donnell brought us in. Up 'til now she had been pretty nice and hadn't yelled, but I could see a storm coming and we deserved it.

"This is a 3v1. Three of you should be able to beat one defender and get a good shot off. The idea is to move the ball to a space where there is no defender. Remember, it takes more than one player to beat a defense. Now, go back and see if you can fix it."

Jeez, I had been expecting a major blow up. That's what our softball coach used to do when we were messing up. I have to say, Ms. O'Donnell stayed pretty cool, but it was definitely an "I mean business and expect you to do it" kind of cool. Even though she didn't raise her voice, I could hear the snap in her talk and the glint in her eyes. I sure hoped I never got on her bad side.

I guess other people saw it too because we did get better, but there were still some girls who didn't pass the ball. It seemed to me that we all had a long way to go to play smart hockey, and I wondered for the first time if it was going to take more than a drill to make us play like a team.

At the end of practice, Jules and I were waiting to pick up our shirts and I said to her, "Hard practice today, but I liked it."

"I wish some people would stop hogging the ball," she said.

I agreed with her, but I didn't think there was anything we could do about it so I changed the subject. "What do you think about Katie Hart not making the team?"

"Jackie, to be honest, I love K to death, but she was really slow. She barely played on our eighth grade team. I'm more concerned about Kate Ross. She really seemed down in practice today."

"I know. I hope this won't make her want to give up hockey." The conversation made me think about how making a team could affect a friendship, and when I got on the bus I realized it was a little emptier than yesterday. It hit me that making a team could make some people feel a little empty, too.

Sitting around the dining room table later that night, everyone congratulated me for making the team, even my mom. Then Lizzie asked me if our uniform was pretty.

I laughed. "I don't know about that part, squirt, but it'll be navy and white."

"I guess all the runs up Browman's Hill really paid off," Dad said.

I grinned and thought about all those hot summer days when I wanted to do anything but climb that hill. Now I knew it had all been worth it.

"I should get in great shape running back and forth between two games, yours and your brother's," Mom added, laughing.

"Speaking of games, Matt said, "We open next Friday night under the lights against Mullica Hill. It was a close one last year, and we were lucky to get away with a win."

"I think we should all go," Dad suggested. "What do you think, Lizzie?"

"Daddy, it's Emily's birthday party next Friday. You promised," Lizzie whined in her 'I want my own way' voice. The only difference was that she wasn't batting her eyes like she usually did. *You're slipping, kid.*

"I'll talk to her mother," Mom said. "Maybe you can stay at Emily's after the party until the game is over." *Okay, Lizzie has graduated from eye batting to whining, but the whole thing is still working. How does she do it?*

"It's settled then," Dad said. "Okay with you, Jackie?"

"I guess."

Looking across the table to Matt, Dad said, "It looks like all your rooters will be there."

That night, I got on my computer and sent an instant message to the twins.

jacmcshootr: r u going 2 the opening boys soccer game next fri

gemsrok: jules and i talked about it a lil. football is away next weekend

boys socr will be our 1st big home game since coming to hs!!!

i think we should get as many players from the team 2 go as we can

we can make it our 1st team get-2-gether

jacmcshootr: good idea! i cant wait

gemrok: g2g study

I signed off and started putting things in my backpack for the next morning. I realized I hadn't been all that keen on going to Matt's game with my mom and dad. It was funny; last year it seemed okay to go to the high school with my parents and cheer for Matt. Now that I was in high school myself, I felt differently about it.

I didn't want anyone thinking I was like some loser little kid, sitting at the game with my parents. But more than that, I just needed to be with my friends. Maybe getting a ride from my parents, then taking off to be with the team would be the way to go. I wondered if my parents would be okay about it.

-8-

The next afternoon in the locker room, I went to get my hockey stick out of the barrel in the equipment room. I searched through the remaining sticks and it wasn't there. I checked every stick again, and then I started to panic. *Did I take it home? Had I left it on the field yesterday?* I was sure I had put it in the barrel after practice the day before.

Other girls came in to get their sticks, and soon I was the only person left. I was going to be late for practice. I went through everything in the equipment room and checked some old open lockers, but they were empty. Just when I was going to give up, I looked under the lockers. There was my stick. I quickly grabbed it and hurried outside.

As I ran to the field, I thought there was no way I put that stick under a locker. Someone had put it there on purpose. The girls were already doing their stick work when I got to the field. Ms. O'Donnell looked up, called me over and asked why I was late.

I explained that I couldn't find my stick, but she wasn't too sympathetic, telling me I needed to be more responsible. Then she sent me on a run as a punishment for being late. As

I ran around the outside of the field, I could see my teammates peeking over at me from time to time, and that made it even worse. I tried to keep my head up, but it was hard. I felt my throat tightening up, making it harder to breathe. I **so** wanted to know who had taken my stick.

Once I finished my run and joined the team, Ms. O'Donnell went on with the rest of practice like nothing had happened, but I felt like I had let her down. I really wanted to get somebody.

Midway through the practice, Ms. O'Donnell told us we would be working on two attacking pieces of the game, penalty corners and penalty strokes. She took Jules, Sam, and me to one end of the field while the others were practicing their jab tackles and assigned each of us a job for penalty corners.

Sam was to start the play by passing the ball out to Jules, who had a real strong hit to goal. My job was to deflect Jules' shot around the goalie. While Ms. O'Donnell was showing Sam how she wanted it done, Jules asked why I had been late. I told her what happened and Jules gave Sam a strange look. I didn't have time to ask her what she was thinking 'cause just then Ms. O'Donnell started explaining what she wanted Jules and me to do.

I tried to do my best, but I kept messing up since I was still thinking about the beginning of practice. Finally, I calmed down and the corners started going pretty well, but then Sam started bellyaching to Coach that maybe she should take the hit instead of Jules 'cause she thought she was really good at scoring, too. I was kind of relieved when Ms. O'Donnell told her to leave it the way it was.

I wished Sam would just shut up about herself and do what Ms. O'Donnell wanted. I was seriously beginning to think that Sam was trying to make our team the Sam Jones Show.

Later on, the whole team practiced penalty strokes. In case you never heard about that one, a player taking a penalty stroke needed to be able to push or lift a stationary ball that had been placed on a mark seven yards from the goal line. It was really like a 1v1 with the goalie, but once the official blew her whistle and the attacker took the stroke, she couldn't approach the goalkeeper. It was kind of like a penalty kick in soccer.

Ms. O'Donnell told us that anyone could try it and she would pick the top five. It turned out that Jules and Anna were deadly strokers and were the two obvious choices to take a stroke in a game. Sam was pretty good too when she was on, but she kind of blew hot and cold; I noticed she got all upset if the goalie stopped her shot. I was the fifth one picked. I didn't know why I was even chosen because I was really struggling to get the ball in the air like the others did.

Ms. O'Donnell came up to me while the others were getting a water break and said, "You know, Jackie, the ball doesn't have to go in the air. You just have to be very accurate and put the ball in the corners of the cage. Just keep practicing and you'll become good at it. I know it."

Well, when your coach said she knew you could do something, especially when you had kind of been on her bad side for being late, that was a pretty big deal, especially if you believed in your coach. So, I was determined to make myself good.

Near the end of practice that day, Ms. O'Donnell brought us in together and said, "There are only two more practices before our first scrimmage. Tomorrow we will practice defensive corners and then go and see part of the varsity game. To finish today's practice, you are all going to do a partner run. It will be a twenty-five minute run together around the outside of the field. Don't pick a person from your old school."

Anna grabbed me and asked to be my partner. I was kind of surprised, but quickly agreed. This was the first time I was doing something away from my old teammates. During the run, we started talking.

"So how do you think we're doing?" I asked. I was curious about what someone else thought outside my close friends.

She thought for a minute. "Okay, but I think we could be a lot better."

"How do you mean?"

"I don't know; I just don't feel like we're a team yet."

"Maybe things will be different when our games start," I said, but I had some doubts even as the words came out of my mouth.

"I hope so," Anna said.

I liked talking to Anna. She was the kind of person who made people around her feel, I don't know, comfortable, I guess you would say.

"Can I ask you something, Anna?"

She nodded.

"What's the deal on Sam? She seems, you know, a little hard to play with."

Anna laughed. "You noticed, huh? She's tough, but she wants to win, Jackie. I think that's why we all put up with her for so long back at our old school."

I thought about the wanting to win stuff, which was all good, but to be honest, Sam was getting on my last nerve, which was not usually how I felt about people.

Later in the locker room, Lindsay came up to me and said, "How come you ran with her?"

I just shrugged my shoulders. I asked her, "Why, don't you like her?"

"I don't know, I guess. Sometimes I just want things to be like they were at Washington."

I kind of understood what she meant, but I was beginning to learn that things couldn't stay that way anymore, whether we liked it or not. I was taking my backpack out of my locker when Lindsay said, "I think Kate Ross is going to quit."

That shocked me. "We have to stop her," I said. "She's a really good player and gets along with everyone. Maybe we can talk to her while we wait for the late buses."

I walked over to Jules and told her what Lindsay had said. Jules stopped gathering up her gear and looked at me. "We could try," she said, but I could tell from the tone of her voice that she wasn't sure we could do much good.

Lindsay, Jules, and I waited for Kate to dress and then we all walked outside together to board the late buses.

"Kate," Jules said, putting some enthusiasm in her voice, "we were thinking about going to the soccer game next Friday as a team. Want to come? It would be fun!"

"I don't know. I've been kind of thinking that I should focus on my schoolwork more and maybe not play hockey," she said.

Jules tried again. "We know you miss Katie, but remember all the fun we had last year having spaghetti dinners the nights before our home games, decorating the buses, and going to the Haunted Hayride together at Aberdeen Farms?"

Kate gave us a little smile like her old self. "It was fun, but this year things seem so different."

I felt in my gut that Kate was already drifting away from us, and I said the only thing I could think of. "We would really miss you. Think about it, okay?"

"I will. Bye," she said as she started walking to her bus.

I looked at Jules and Lindsay. "What do you think?"

"I don't know. We tried, Jackie," Jules said.

Lindsay headed to the bus Kate had boarded. I was hoping that they could keep talking and that Lindsay could convince Kate to stay with the team. It sure wasn't going to be the same season as last year, that was for sure.

On Friday, the team focused on defensive penalty corners. The attack's job was just to give them practice while the defense worked on their positioning. Sam continued to be sulky about her job being the passer for the attack and not the chief scorer. She purposely hit poor passes to make us mess up when Coach wasn't looking, and I just wanted to slap her. I didn't know how we were ever going to be a good team with her attitude. I sure hoped she wasn't going to act that way in a game.

After we'd done our corners, Ms. O'Donnell brought us in and told us to put all of our things on the bleachers. She was taking us over to the varsity field to watch some of the varsity scrimmage. She thought it would give us some good ideas on how to play in our scrimmage on Tuesday.

When we arrived, the second half was just starting. I looked at the scoreboard, but it was blank, and I guessed it wasn't lit up because it was a scrimmage. It didn't take long, however, for us to realize that Northfield was the stronger team.

I turned to Lindsay sitting next to me. "Wow, look how fast they move the ball! They make us look so slow."

"The defense is totally awesome," she said without letting her eyes leave the field. "They're stopping all of the other team's through passes."

At one point, the ball went out the sidelines, where we were sitting, and a varsity player came over to start the in bounds play. She looked up at Lindsay and snapped, "Hey freshman, how about getting the ball instead of just sitting there."

Lindsay gave her a stony look, but she got up and went under the bleachers to get the ball anyway and flipped it to the girl. The player just turned away and didn't even say thanks. Maybe the girl was too wrapped up in getting the play going to think of it, but I didn't think the girl was very nice. How long did it take to say "thanks?"

After a moment, we kind of forgot about it, and within the next fifteen minutes, Northfield had scored three goals. I have to say, the varsity was pretty impressive, at least on the field, and watching the game psyched us up for our own scrimmage. Once we got back to the freshman field, though, that feeling lasted only a few minutes 'cause Ms. O'Donnell ended our practice with some killer wind sprints.

We were walking back to the locker room when Jules said, "We're going to be like that someday."

Tori laughed. "Maybe we'll be better."

"They make it look so easy," I said.

Ms. O'Donnell was walking right behind us and must have overheard our conversation because she said, "You know, they were like you at one time, but with hard work and dedication they got a lot better, and you can too. Maybe in a couple of years, I will bring another freshman team to a scrimmage and watch you play." Then she gave a little smile. "In the meantime, let's get our fundamentals down and become a good team this year."

She may not have realized it, but Ms. O'Donnell had just given us a peek into our future. I can tell you, I was super hyped just thinking about it.

Saturday morning I woke up late and lay in bed for a while, thinking about my first days at Northfield. I'd found my classes and pretty much knew my way around school, which was a real plus 'cause two weeks ago I had been a total wreck about it. I still had most of my friends from eighth grade, and I'd met some cool new people, too, like Anna and Kerry. Anna was really easy to talk to, and I thought we could become good friends. Sam Jones, of course, was something else again. Why couldn't the girl play tennis, or anything besides hockey?

Then some other new faces drifted into my mind. One of them was that Mitch Kennedy guy. I had to admit, he seemed pretty nice for a boy. And I wasn't blind; he was good looking, not that it mattered, but maybe we could get to be friends. Not boyfriend stuff, not that he would be interested, of course. Just friends.

I sure never wanted all the drama with a boy that I saw some of the girls go through last year. Eighth grade was a mess with someone always getting their feelings hurt, crying in the bathroom at dances, and for what? One girl even fought another girl over a boy. Ridiculous stuff! Some of those boys were clearly jerks. Boyfriends could cause a whole lot of pain; that was for sure.

Now, I knew that not all boys were goon balls 'cause my brother was great. Maybe when I was a junior or senior and I met someone like Matt it would be fun to have a boyfriend. *Why am I even thinking like this? Just because Mitch talked to me doesn't mean he would ever think of me like that. I'm getting all worked up over nothing.* I rolled over and pulled the sheet up around me. *Boy stuff is just too much trouble!*

Sometimes, I imagined that starting out in high school must be like reading a new book and that I was just starting chapter one. You kind of knew that things were going to happen, but what, who, when? And the back of the book was sealed shut so you couldn't sneak a peek at the ending to see how things turned out. A little frustrating, if you thought about it too long.

Later that morning, I had finished the list of chores my mom had left for me and I decided to call the twins.

"What are you guys up to?"

"We're going to the library for a couple of hours this afternoon," Jules said. "I have a paper due next Friday and I want to get it done, and Tori is taking an art course and needs to look at some books there. Want to come along? Our mom is going to take us."

"I don't know."

"Oh, come on, Jackie, you can get some homework done and then we can walk over to the mall until five o'clock when our mom will pick us up."

Thoughts of going to a library sounded boring to me, even if I was hanging there with my best friends. I sighed. "No, I'll pass. Maybe some other time."

"Okay," Jules said. "See you Monday."

How can I explain about me and schoolwork? I always did my homework; I just did it as fast as I could. I was too antsy to pay much attention in class, and really, most of it was so boring. I just wanted to be out on the hockey field. Maybe there was a professional field hockey school somewhere, a place with no teachers, just coaches and lots of green grass, and no boys, either, 'cause they could distract you and make you think of stuff other than hockey. That would be my kind of school.

-9-

On Monday morning in homeroom, Mitch leaned forward and said, "I think we're having a pop quiz in world history today. Did you study the chapter on ancient Egypt?"

"Sort of," I replied. *Actually, that would be a pretty big no.* "I'll go over it in study hall, thanks."

"It's an easy class, Jackie, and you want to get a good grade."

I turned around and looked at him, kind of surprised. "I didn't think you cared all that much about grades. You seem all casual about things." *And way too cool.*

"My dad expects me to ace my classes. It's sort of a given."

"What's your dad do?"

"He's in the military, stationed at McGuire Air Force Base."

"Oh," I said. I'd never even met anyone who had a parent in the military. Maybe my first impression of Mitch as being a bit of a wise guy was way off. The bell rang and I smiled at Mitch. "See you later, Mitch, and thanks for the heads up."

When I opened my history book in study hall, all I could think was, *Thank goodness Mitch Kennedy told me about the quiz. I barely looked at the chapter.*

See, I'd always gotten by without working too hard. I figured I could slide through high school doing the same amount of work and still get okay grades. You need to know that in my group of friends, the twins are major brains and far out of my ballpark. I couldn't even imagine being in the same league with them when it came to the academic stuff. Digging into my history book, I realized that I'd never given too much thought to grades at all, and as long as I had been in the middle somewhere, my mom and dad hadn't said too much.

It was pretty amazing to me that someone like Mitch Kennedy was so on top of preparing for a little pop quiz. *Maybe it should be more important to work on getting better grades. All right, I have forty minutes to review these twelve pages.*

That afternoon, sure enough, there was a pop quiz in world history. When Mr. Coles went over the answers, I realized that I'd gotten only two wrong out of twenty. *Thank you, Mitchell Kennedy!* I would have definitely blown it if it wasn't for him.

After class when we were walking out the door, I said to him, "You bailed me out on that one. I owe you."

He looked down at me and winked. "Don't worry. I can find ways for you to pay me back."

His comment suddenly made me feel uncomfortable. It was not the words so much as how he said them. I didn't expect it, and I didn't have a clever comeback. He kept looking at my face, which I was sure was as red as my hair, and then he reached out and ruffled my hair.

How did I respond? Like an idiot, I shoved him into the wall.

"Hey, Jackie, I was just playing," he laughed, rubbing his arm, pretending like I really hurt him.

I could tell he was trying to keep things light 'cause he kept the conversation going. "Seriously, Jackie, when it comes to academics, I know that my dad being on my back is what got me to start doing well in school, but I do get that it's important. My older sister is in her final year at Vanderbilt, and she is going on to graduate school next year. She wants a career in medical research."

"I didn't know you had a sister."

It turned out he had two sisters. I wondered if the other one went to Northfield, but he said she was back in Texas. "That's where my dad was stationed for a while. We've all gone to a bunch of different schools with my dad in the military, but when my dad got transferred here this summer, my sister put her foot down and my mom agreed. Megan, that's my younger sister, is a senior in high school, and she wanted to finish out school with her class. Besides, she's a basketball player there and it was important for her to be with her team."

"How come you didn't stay there too?"

"I'm hoping to start and finish at the same high school, and I kind of thought my dad could use some company. Next summer I'll go back to Texas and see my mom and sisters. My dad will stay here. He'll retire out at McGuire."

Before I knew it, we were in front of the entrance to the girls' locker room. *Did he actually just walk me here?*

He smiled down at me. "I'm going to go shoot some hoops. Have a good practice, Jackie."

"See you later," I said as I turned into the locker room. For a moment, I forgot it had really bothered me when he messed up my hair like he did. Of course, if I had my ponytail, he couldn't have done that. *Thanks a lot, Mom!*

I was moving slowly, thinking about my longest conversation ever with a boy, and it wasn't so bad. I was sitting on the bench, stupid like, not paying much attention to anything, and for once I wasn't rushing to get out on the field for practice. I must have been in a fog 'cause all of a sudden, I heard Tori call over to me, "Hey, wake up; it's almost three o'clock." I looked up, realized the time and quickly got changed. I had to sprint to get to practice on time.

After practice, Tori came up to me. "You all right?"

"What do you mean?"

"You just looked kind of out of it in the locker room, that's all. I wondered if something bad had happened today."

"No, nothing like that. I think that maybe I need to talk to you...boy stuff."

Tori raised an eyebrow as if she was surprised by what I said but didn't want to let on. At least she didn't laugh out loud about why I would be asking anything about a boy. She just acted like typical Tori, all flip and funny.

"Well, you've come to the expert," she laughed. "You know, I spend most of my day just plotting and planning about guys."

That was the truth! Tori had never been shy in the boy department. She had already been 'in love' more times than you could count.

After dinner, I went up to my room and made my mind up to finish my math and science homework before I called Tori. I decided that maybe I needed to be a little more disciplined in using my time for schoolwork. Okay, that was a lie. I was really getting wet feet, and I was trying to postpone talking to Tori.

When I finished up my assignments, I glanced at the clock. It was almost nine. I thought that maybe I shouldn't bother Tori since it was so late, but then I figured Tori would probably wonder why I didn't call. I picked up the phone.

"I'm not too late, am I?" I asked as Tori got on the line.

"No, it's fine. What's going on?"

"Well, there's this guy in my homeroom, Mitch Kennedy."

Tori got all excited. Her antenna was up. "Is he tall and athletic looking with spiky dark hair?"

"That's him."

"He's a hottie, Jackie; he's in my Spanish II class. The girls are seriously checking him out."

I frowned. *Why does that bother me? What should I expect, anyway, that I should be the only girl in the world who notices him?*

"Jackie," Tori went on, "if you're interested in him, you better make a move before somebody else grabs him."

"I don't know if I **am** interested," I snapped. *Jeez, this discussion is getting complicated.*

Tori paused for a minute, like she was trying to figure out what to say next. "Well, do you think he's interested in you?"

"I don't know. How can you tell?" I was starting to think that maybe I shouldn't have even mentioned Mitch at all. I was definitely stepping on that invisible line that could cause me some trouble. Then I sighed and thought, *What the heck, this is just a conversation between me and my bud,* and I said, "Well, he talks to me, but maybe he's just being friendly."

"Jackie, can I say something?"

"I guess."

"Boys have always liked you. You just haven't been looking before. Seriously, Jackie, you are a real fun person to be with and one of the nicest people I know. Why wouldn't he be interested? Besides, you've certainly got it in the looks department and you act like it's no big deal. Guys like that. I think the first thing you've got to decide is if you are interested in him. Meanwhile, I'll do some detective work and find out if he's into you at all."

"Oh, don't do that, Tori," I pleaded.

"Don't worry, I'll be clever. He won't suspect a thing."

"Okay," I said reluctantly. I was starting to feel like I was getting in way over my head.

"Listen, Jackie, I've got to get my homework done and get to bed. We've got a scrimmage tomorrow. Don't worry about this, okay?"

How can I not worry? I thought, but I said, "See you tomorrow, and thanks, Tori."

"What are friends for, right, Jackie?"

After Tori hung up, I was wondering what in the world I was doing. *I was crazy to talk to Tori. So, other girls like Mitch Kennedy. So what? Was that really my business? I'm making my life way too complicated. I should just stick to hockey.* With all these thoughts whirling around in my head, I tried to drift off to sleep.

On Tuesday morning, I stood in front of my closet for a long time deciding what to wear, or maybe I was deciding something else. Sometimes, it's hard to figure out what a person's thoughts are really about, especially your own.

Finally, I picked out a dark green sweater that I hardly ever wore. I thought it might look good with my red hair. Getting into gear, I tore through my dresser drawer for the unused cosmetic bag my mom had given me for my fourteenth birthday, which I had thrown in the drawer after my birthday was over. I rooted around in the bag to see what was in there. I had no idea what I was looking for; it was totally a grab bag of mysterious clutter.

I stared at myself in the bathroom mirror. *What am I doing? Is this really me, the make-up stuff? Am I being fake just so someone might like me?* I remembered Jules reacting to my haircut and saying how high school was a time to try something new, and I knew the right way to go. It wasn't like I was putting on permanent tattoos. If I didn't like the new me, I could just forget about it.

I found some lip gloss and blush and began to experiment. At first I put on too much blush and looked like a clown. I washed it off, and after one more try, it did look better. I checked myself in the mirror one last time before going downstairs to make sure I didn't look too stupid. *See, Mom, you got your wish; I've finally used this stuff.*

At breakfast, my mom looked at me and smiled. I prayed, *DON'T SAY ANYTHING! Pretend I look normal.* She must have been a mind reader 'cause she was doing a pretty good job of ignoring my face. She went on unloading the dishwasher like it was just any old morning.

I looked at myself in the hall mirror one last time before catching the bus. *It's still me. I'm just taking it up a notch; it's no big deal to look a little nice for school, right?*

No, I'm being ridiculous trying so hard to look nice. I bounded back up the stairs, threw the sweater on the floor and grabbed a T-shirt out of the drawer. I looked at my watch, but there wasn't time to wash my face.

In homeroom, I pretended to look busy with my head buried in a book when Mitch came in. I could sense the clock ticking and knew I had to face him. If he laughed, I thought I would die. Finally, I worked up the courage to look at him and I turned around in my chair.

"How was basketball yesterday?"

He got all wide eyed and said, "You look really nice, Jackie."

"Oh, thanks," I said, kind of off handedly. Secretly, I was relieved I had passed the no-clown test and maybe a little sorry my green sweater was lying on the floor.

He went on talking, like compliments from boys and me in make-up were just everyday events and not something earth shattering.

"Basketball is going pretty well," he said. "The coach said they're starting 'open gym' three days a week after school. It's only for an hour, but it's good for getting to know how people work and sizing up the competition."

"So you're going out for the team?"

"Yeah, but we can't officially start 'til November first."

I asked if he was any good with a straight face. I mean, I figured he was so tall and all that he must be good. Plus his hands…well, they were like two catcher's mitts. I bet he could have even palmed the basketball.

I think my question kind of took him aback for a moment —how could anyone think he wasn't good? — but then he looked into my eyes, and that probably gave me away. He knew I was just teasing him.

He grinned at me and said, "Oh, yeah." He reached out and grabbed my fingers that were lying across the back of my chair and gave them a playful squeeze. I felt something shift inside the pit of my stomach. *Jackie, girl, what **are** you getting yourself into?* As I turned around in my seat, I knew the color in my cheeks was just not from the morning's make-up job.

In world history, I let Mr. Coles know I had to leave twenty minutes early for an away scrimmage, and he told me to make sure I got the work I would miss from someone in class.

How was I going to do that? I don't even know anyone in this class. On the way back to my seat, I looked at Mitch and it struck me. I asked him if he could let me know what went on in class.

"No problem. Give me your number and I'll phone you tonight. How late can I call you?"

"Anytime up to 9:30 is okay. That's when my sister goes to bed."

I started to sit down and I heard Mitch laugh. "And your number is?"

"Oh, right." I blushed and I gave it to him.

I watched him write it down in his notebook, and when I was leaving, he touched my back lightly and wished me luck.

-10-

It was fun to be getting on a bus with a team again, going to a game. Even though it was only a scrimmage it was still about us versus them, you know, THE TEST. It was like finding out if you still had it, if you had done the work to make it happen. Even though I was still pretty young, I knew in my bones it was what made life roll along.

Everyone was very chatty on the ride, but as I looked around, the girls were mostly sitting with their teammates from last year. The exception was our goalies. Becky and Kerry were together, shoulder to shoulder, and I could hear Becky, who was still out, pumping up Kerry for the game. Goalies on a team are either silent enemies 'cause they're both going after something that only one of them can have, or they are this awesome little team that totally has each other's backs. I thought Kerry and Becky were going to be this kind of team. I hoped the rest of us could be like that, too.

Once we arrived at the school, we went to the locker room. Everyone was a little nervous, and the one thing you don't want to do is hear the whistle blow and then have to use the facilities, you know what I mean?

We started to go through our warm up, but I was thinking that something was missing. We did everything we were supposed to, but there was no fire. I smelled trouble. Ms. O'Donnell brought us in and gave us the starting lineup.

The forwards were me, Sam Jones, and another girl from Morrisville named Sarah Graff. The mid-field attackers were Tori and Heather Whitcraft, a little blond from Gibbstown I was excited to have as a teammate 'cause she was a real fighter. The three midfield defenders, to no one's surprise, were Jules, Lindsay, and Anna. The deep backs were another girl from Gibbstown named Caitlin Grant and Ellen. Kerry, of course, was playing in the goal. Ms. O'Donnell told us that our main job for the day was to give good direction to each other on the field.

As the half got underway, our team came up with the ball a lot, but we didn't make much progress down the field. When the other team got possession of the ball, our defenders held strong, but it seemed that our passing to each other was way off. It was basically like Gibbstown passed to Gibbstown, Washington to Washington, and Morrisville to Morrisville. Whatever happened to passing to an open player? Every time Sam got the ball she either kept it herself or passed it to the other forward, never to me.

Tori noticed it too and yelled out, "Sam, Jackie's open!"

"I didn't see her," Sam muttered back.

I was thinking that maybe I should make an appointment for her at our local Four Eyes for glasses. Of course, that wasn't the only thing I was thinking.

After fifteen minutes of play, Ms. O'Donnell shook up the lineup a little bit, subbing Kate Ross for Ellen and Steph Jankowski for the right wing, Sarah. The defense sent some good hard passes to Steph and she flew down the field after the ball, but maybe 'cause it was her first year playing hockey, she didn't do much with the ball once she got it. I moved down the field with her and I felt we had kind of got a rhythm going. Once she had more skill, we'd work well together, unlike me and some other forward that I won't name.

At halftime, the score was 0-0. Ms. O'Donnell brought us into the huddle, and she was way more intense than she had ever been before. She banged her pen on the clipboard as she spoke, and I could hear her frustration.

"It is not enough to have the best speed or the best stick skills," she started, and then she revved it up another notch. "We have dominated possession of the ball, but we are still not able to move the ball down the field as a team. We have taken only two shots and have had no corners. We need to get better fast. I am putting in the people who did not start the first half. I want the rest of you to watch."

The other coach seemed to have subbed players, too, since play in the second half started out slow for both teams. In the first fifteen minutes, neither team took a shot. All of us on the bench were quiet, just watching and waiting to see what our coach would do with us. We sure knew she wasn't happy. I was thinking that I just wanted to go back in and prove to her that we could do better.

Finally, both coaches subbed back their original lineups. Now our team was dominating again, and things started to get better for us. Tori and Heather stepped up with quick interceptions and got some good shots off, causing the other team to foul.

We got three attacking corners in a row, but the shots were either fumbled or went wide of the cage. Still, for the next ten minutes, we were able to keep the ball at our attacking end of the field. Finally, Lindsay got her stick on the ball and sent a long drive from the center of the field toward the goal. I read the hit and took off toward the striking circle. Just as the other team's goalie was about to stop the hit, I tipped the ball around her and it flew into the corner.

Our celebration didn't last, though. With time running down on the clock, an attacker from the other team intercepted a sloppy pass between two of our defenders and sent a dribbling shot toward Kerry. It could have been an easy save, but I was worried because Kerry had been standing around not doing anything for a long time. I cringed, waiting to see what would happen. Sure enough, as soon as Kerry went to play the ball it rolled under her kickers and into the goal. Ten seconds later, the scrimmage was over.

It was very quiet going home on the bus. The team knew we had disappointed Ms. O'Donnell as well as ourselves. When the bus pulled into the Northfield High School parking lot, Ms. O'Donnell stood up at the front of the bus, turned to us, and said, "I think we all realize that this performance today does not represent our athletic talent or skill. However, it does indicate our progress as a team, which I would say is not very much. Tonight I want each of you to think about what you need to be doing to make us a stronger team. Believe me, I will be doing it too. See you tomorrow."

She looked at every single person on the bus as she was speaking. It was as though she was pinning us to the wall with every word. We could hear the determination, and knew that things were not going to stay the same if she had anything to say about it. It made you want to play that much harder.

At dinner, my mom asked how the game went, and I told her we tied 1-1.

"That's good, honey."

"No, Mom, it isn't good. We didn't play well at all."

"Well, maybe the next game will be better, Jackie," she said. *She so doesn't get it.*

"Mommy," Lizzie chirped up, "our class is going to the zoo tomorrow, and today we drew pictures of our favorite animals in art. I like the lions the best, like in *The Lion King.*"

"Lizzie, your trip will be so much fun. Tonight we'll go on the computer and look up some things about lions."

The conversation continued around the table, but I tuned it out. I was still thinking about the afternoon's scrimmage. *Why couldn't I have helped the team more? What can I possibly say at practice tomorrow?*

After dinner I called the twins. Jules answered and asked if I was feeling as bad as she was.

"Yeah, but I don't know what is going on. I don't think the attack is doing the job. Maybe I shouldn't be out there."

"Jackie, don't be ridiculous. You are the best attacker on the team. You're just not getting the ball. Look, the defense did an okay job stopping the ball, sure. And that goal of theirs was just a fluke. But the defense has to do a better job of helping the attack because we are just not being smart. We're not working as a team to get you guys more chances to score."

"How are we going to do that?" I said.

"I'm not sure, but we need to do something. Maybe the team should sit down and talk."

"Maybe," I said, but I was a little doubtful that talking was going to do much good. "Well, I have to go read my book for English. See you tomorrow, Jules."

"Yeah, Jackie, hang tough; it'll get better."

For once, I wasn't so sure I agreed with her.

I puffed up the pillows on my bed and lay back, ready to spend the next hour reading my English assignment. I was pretty surprised by how much I liked the book 'cause I usually wasn't into reading much. It was Ernest Gaines' story about this amazing woman, Miss Jane Pitman.

Before I realized it, I was getting all wrapped up in the story, forgetting the time. Around nine o'clock the phone rang, and Mom called up, "It's for you, Jackie."

I picked up the extension in my room. "Hi," I said without really thinking, the story still swirling in my mind.

"Hello to you, Reds," said a strange male voice. I was stunned. It was Mitch Kennedy. I didn't know what to say. "How was the game?" he asked, probably since I wasn't giving him anything to go on and he had to say something.

"Uh, okay I guess. Can you hold on a minute?" Not waiting for his answer, I put down the phone and quickly rummaged through my backpack for some gum. All of a sudden my mouth had gotten kind of dry and needed some backup. Chomping on the gum, I felt a little better.

"Sorry about that. Actually, we tied 1-1."

"Was it a good tie or a bad tie?" he asked.

I smiled to myself. *He knows the right question to ask. He totally understands.* "We should've played a lot better."

"How did you do?"

"I scored, but I didn't really get the ball much."

"How come? Don't they pass the ball to you?"

"No, not a lot. It's kind of frustrating."

"That's tough, Jackie. It can happen in basketball too."

I rolled onto my side and nestled into my pillow. "So Mitch, did anything special happen in world history?"

"Nah, I took some notes. I'll give you a copy tomorrow. I just called because I like to hear your voice. You can phone me too, you know." Not even giving me a chance to ask why, he went on. "Here's my number." As he gave it to me, I quickly grabbed a pencil and wrote it on the inside of my book.

"So what's going on this weekend, Jackie?" *What's that supposed to mean?* I got up and started pacing around the room.

"Anything happening at school?" he said. I paused and let out a breath. *Chill.*

"On Friday night, I think the hockey team is going to meet up at the soccer game. My brother plays," I said, finally stringing two sentences together, almost like a real conversation,

"What year's your brother?"

"Matt's a senior; he's pretty good. He has college people coming to see him play."

"That's cool. Maybe I'll see you there," he said. "I guess I better let beauty get her sleep. See you tomorrow, Jackie."

He called, he called, he called! I couldn't take the smile off my face as I put back the phone and slipped under the covers. After a minute or two, my jaw actually started aching from all the smiling. *Wait 'til I tell Tori.* Then I gradually came off my high. *What am I getting so excited about? I asked him to call. Anyway, he's just a boy in my class, right?*

At breakfast the next morning, Mom asked, "Who was the boy who called last night?"

Down periscope, dive, dive! Mom's radar screen had just been activated, and I sure didn't need her tracking this one.

"Oh, just a student from class giving me some notes I missed," I said, trying to shoot a decoy into the water to throw her off track.

Slurping away at her cereal Lizzie said, "Jackie's got a boyfriend."

That brought my dad's nose out of the sports page. Zeroing in on me in lightning speed, he asked, "What's that?"

"It's nothing," I said.

"His name is Mitch, he —"

"Lizzie!" I turned on her in a flash. *The little monster must have been listening in. I thought she was busy getting ready for bed. I so need a room of my own!*

"What's going on, Jackie?" said Dad, getting even more focused on the conversation.

"He's just a guy from school. I hardly know him."

"Well, if someone is under the impression he is going to date my daughter, I want to meet him. Do you understand me, Jackie?"

"Okay, but this isn't anything like that," I said. I felt like I was slipping into a giant sinkhole or something. Mom just looked at Dad with one of those all-knowing mother looks. *Some secret parental sign language is going on*, I thought. On the way to the bus I began to wonder, *Is there a place in this world where a girl can grow up without her family in her business?*

In homeroom, Mitch handed me the notes from world history, and as I looked at the pages, I realized they were actually notes from the entire class period. "Wow, Mitch, you take good notes. They're so neat and organized."

"I'll let you in on my secret," he grinned. "I've got horrible handwriting; I always copy my notes over. It helps me study better."

"Thanks. These are great."

"I didn't keep you up too late, did I?" he asked.

"No, but my snoopy little sister gave a shout out to my parents at breakfast."

He laughed. "I ratted on my sisters when I was younger, too. I can't believe I'm even still alive."

I suddenly relaxed. I found myself studying him, imagining him at eight or nine, and said, "I bet you were a demon when you were little."

He grinned back at me. "I'm sure my sisters thought so." The bell rang, and as we headed out, Mitch actually winked at me and said, "See you later."

Even though I was on my way to Spanish, I wondered if I should take a detour to the nurse's office to see if she had a defibrillator 'cause my heart was beating kind of weird just then. I knew I needed to stop feeling like that, all unnatural and strange, but I sure didn't have an answer on how to do it.

-12-

The Table at lunch was getting a little more crowded. While I was munching on my customary slice of pizza, Anna came up to the table and asked if it was okay for Kerry and her to sit with us.

Jules gave a nod and smiled, but just to be sure, I asked Britt and Alisha if they minded. Now, this was an important lunch table procedure to follow, to actually ask, 'cause memberships at lunch tables have to be mutually okayed by the whole group.

Everyone was all good with it, so Jules said, "Put your stuff down and grab something to eat. Maybe we can all put our heads together and talk about yesterday's game."

While we ate, we started reviewing the previous day's scrimmage. "What do you think about yesterday, Kerry?" Jules asked. "You get a great view of things back there?"

"First I want to apologize for letting that ball go into the cage. I feel so stupid," Kerry said. She was looking down at the table and I felt bad for her. It had to be hard being a goalie.

"Don't feel that way," I said. "Sometimes shots are hard to judge, especially when you've been standing with no action for a long time."

"She's right, Kerry," Jules said. "Anyway, that is not why we didn't win. We're just not playing together as a team. We don't see who is open."

"It's not even that," Anna interrupted. "We are only thinking about ourselves or our friends. Some of us are treating our teammates like they don't even exist."

"Hey guys, what's going on?" Lindsay asked, coming up to us and taking in how *The Table* had suddenly increased in size.

"Where have you been?" Britt asked. "You giving up on eating?"

"I should," Lindsay said, looking down at her stomach. "I had an orthodontist appointment this morning, and my mother just dropped me off. Believe me, my mouth is so sore I don't think I could even suck through a straw."

"Come on, sit down," I said and moved over to make room for her. "We were just talking about yesterday."

Plopping her books down on the table, Lindsay said, "I think we just ought to forget about yesterday and move on."

"That's not going to solve anything," Jules said. But Lindsay rolled her eyes and turned away from Jules. I didn't know why the two of them couldn't get along better. On the field they were fine, but once they were done playing, they just seemed to get on each other's nerves for some reason.

"Guys, far be it for me, the non-athlete, to say any-thing," Alisha said carefully, sounding like she wasn't sure she should step into it, "but it seems to me that if you just let your coach know you want things to be better, that could be a starting point."

We all looked at her.

"Alisha, you are totally brilliant. That's it," Jules said, and we made a pact to speak to Ms. O'Donnell at the beginning of practice.

In the locker room, we were all hurrying to get dressed so we would have time to speak to Ms. O'Donnell. Ellen came in a little late and came over to Lindsay and me and said in voice only we could hear, "Kate Ross turned in her equipment today. She quit."

"For sure?" I asked.

"She told me this morning in algebra. She said she just didn't enjoy yesterday enough to stick with it."

"That stinks. She has been playing with us since fifth grade," I said. "I'm sure going to miss her."

"Nothing is staying the same. I wish we could have our old team back the way it was," Lindsay said, almost to herself.

We hustled out to the field, and I saw Jules, Kerry, and Anna already talking with Ms. O'Donnell. When we joined them, Anna was saying, "We talked at lunch, and we think there are a lot of us who want to be a better team and play better than we did yesterday."

Ms. O'Donnell looked at each of us and said, "I'm glad you let me know how you feel. The first step is to desire change. Then the change can happen. I'll bring everyone together before we start our warm up."

Ms. O'Donnell whistled all the other girls over and began to speak to the whole team. She told us that we needed to understand where we were as a team and where we wanted to be. She explained about Kate Ross deciding not to play, which surprised almost everybody, and then she said that we needed to make everyone feel important. We were a bunch of cliques and not one team. What she said made me feel bad, but I knew she was right.

She reminded us that we had a lot more in common with each other than we thought, and she told us we were going to do a little exercise to learn more about each other. That got my curiosity going. There were a lot of girls who were just a name and a position to me, and not much more.

She had us count off in twos and put us in two lines facing each other five yards apart. She joined one of the lines, and then she said, "I've given our manager, Nadja, a list of questions. When she reads each question and the answer pertains to you, I want you to step forward into the middle in a straight line. We'll start out with easy questions. Ready? Go ahead, Nadja."

Nadja started, saying, "Who has a July birthday?" Three girls stepped to the middle line. They looked at each other and quickly asked for birthdates.

"All right, step back," our coach said.

There were a couple more simple questions that got the team loose, and then Nadja asked, "How many of you were really nervous about the first day of high school?"

I looked around and I was surprised to see that most of my teammates had also stepped forward. *Wow, that's pretty amazing. There are so many.* I had to say that even though we were standing there looking a little sheepish, like we were letting the cat out of the bag for the first time, I thought that admitting this in front of each other was a pretty big deal.

Suddenly, Tori turned to the six girls who were still back in their lines. With a big grin on her face, she wiggled her finger at them, saying, "You know you're all lying." The whole team broke up laughing.

The questioning went on. "How many people have ever felt that they were not good enough as a player?" More than a dozen players stepped forward, including me, of course, but also including Ms. O'Donnell. We all looked at our coach in amazement.

Lindsay blurted out, "But you were all-state."

"Ah, I see some of us have been doing some snooping," Ms. O'Donnell laughed. "I was fortunate to have some success as a player, but there were moments when I had some doubts about myself," she said.

"How did you get through them?" asked Heather Whitcraft.

"My teammates helped me out. I always felt like they had my back and I learned to count on them, especially when I was having a bad day."

She paused for a moment, letting her comments sink into our thick heads. Then she said, "Okay, next question, Nadja." After a few more questions, we stopped. The rest of practice went on, but I felt that things were somehow different with the team. The players seemed more relaxed with each other. I sure hoped it continued.

Afterward, I thought about what Ms. O'Donnell had said. She was such a great player, yet she hadn't always been sure of herself either. I sure knew what a lonely feeling it was when you thought you stunk at something. Maybe she was right, and you could count on teammates to get you through. And maybe we needed every one of us to be a team, everyone being there for each other — except, of course, dopey Sam Jones.

Just as I got to the locker room, I remembered something that had nothing to do with field hockey and quickly hurried in the door. *I have to tell Tori about last night's phone call.*

The next day in gym class in the middle of a bunch of soccer drills, Mrs. Fortunato walked up to me and asked how things were going in hockey. I told her that the team was trying to work out some things but I was sure we were going to become a good team. Mrs. Fortunato smiled at me and said, "Good," then moved away.

I was kind of surprised she asked. She never talked hockey in class. In fact, Mrs. Fortunato didn't seem to pay any attention to me at all except maybe to have me work with one of the girls when someone was having a hard time with stuff. It seemed like she enjoyed helping the people who were struggling the most. All they had to do was try, and she would be right there for them. I always thought that coaches only focused on the athletes in their classes. Her way of doing things was a real surprise. Right then, I decided that if I ever made varsity someday, being coached by this lady would be one big chapter in my life book.

That afternoon's scrimmage was a big improvement over the last one. While Sam still kept the ball to herself too much and rarely passed the ball to me, the team worked better together and we had a lot more chances to score. After the game, Ms. O'Donnell told us that we would be getting our uniforms tomorrow so practice would be shorter.

Jules reminded the team, "Don't forget, we'd like to get as many of us as possible to sit together at the boys' soccer game tomorrow night. The varsity game starts at 7:30." I hoped people would show up. Despite the scrimmage, I knew we needed a good bonding night.

-13-

On Friday, everyone at *The Table* was kind of jazzed. It was probably because it was the end of the week and then we had two days of no school. That worked for me, at least.

Britt asked us how we had all played in the scrimmage.

"Sure better than the last one," I said. "We've got to keep it up 'cause we open up next Tuesday. How about you? How are things going with the varsity?"

"Okay, I guess. The varsity is mostly seniors. They really don't talk to me unless they want something. They're really cocky, if you ask me. I hear them talking like they think everyone on their schedule is going to roll over just because we're Northfield and we won the state champion-ship last year. They think they're going to be repeats."

Lindsay looked up from peeling her orange. "Are they that good?"

"I'm not sure. I mean, I'm only a manager, so what do I know about playing? They have torn up everyone in their scrimmages, though. They have their opening game today at Browns Mills, so we'll see." She paused and seemed to be studying something on her tray. Then she looked up and said something that surprised me. "I wish I was with you guys."

We all stopped what we were doing. Britt had our attention now.

She went on. "I'll be glad when you guys move up next year. Hearing you talk makes me realize how lonely it can be with the upperclassmen."

"Don't you like the other manager?" I asked.

"Oh, yeah, she's great. We have a good time together. It's just some of the players. They think they're all that. They make me do things for them all the time like I'm just a gofer."

"Yeah, at their scrimmage, one of them told me to go get the ball for her like I was her personal servant," Lindsay said. "I almost said something like, 'maybe if you were in shape you'd be able to get the ball yourself,' but I behaved."

I laughed 'cause Lindsay definitely had a mouth when it came down to it. "Good control there, Linds."

Lindsay smiled back. "It was close."

"Maybe it's a good thing we're not around them and on our own field," I said.

All the good vibes that had been at our table went south for a moment as everyone thought about the upperclassmen. Then Lindsay turned to me. "So, is Matt psyched about the soccer game tonight?"

"I think so. Matt doesn't talk much about the games until after they've played them. I know a scout is supposed to be coming tonight from some college in Vermont, or New Hampshire, or somewhere, to see him play. I heard my parents talking about it at breakfast."

"Does Matt know he's being scouted?" asked Alisha. "If that was me I would be so nervous."

"He knows a scout will be there. I think he just figures that's what's supposed to happen if you're good. I know he really wants to play in college."

Jules, who had been sitting quietly at the table reviewing for a test, finally stopped her studying. "I know I want to play hockey in college," she said.

"You're thinking about college already?" Lindsay asked.

"Yeah, I really am, at least as far as hockey is concerned," Jules replied. "I know that college ball is my dad's plan for Chris, too."

"Who's Chris?" Anna asked.

"My brother. He's a junior at St. Benedict's. My dad's his high school basketball coach there."

"I didn't know your dad is a coach," Anna said.

"Yep, he coaches 24/7. When Tori and I got to sixth grade and we were already 5'7", everybody assumed we would be playing basketball, but we said no way. Chris could have been a student here, too, but Dad wanted to coach Chris himself. My brother gets all the focus on him, and Tori and I can have a good old time here at Northfield as long as we get good grades."

Anna seemed surprised by what Jules was saying, but I knew the real story. The twins told me in confidence a long time ago. See, Mr. Hanson was some hotshot basketball player a long time ago. He even played in the pro leagues in Europe. Growing up, Chris would always hear, "Oh, you're Don Hanson's kid. Can you hit the basket like your old man?" I thought it must get old, always being compared to your father, not that Chris complained.

Although the twins didn't think they would be hassled as much as their brother since they were girls and all, they still didn't want their father's crazy drive for perfection make them hate playing, so they crossed off basketball and focused on hockey. Their decision was a pretty smart one, if you ask me, 'cause Mr. Hanson knew squat about field hockey so he had to keep his mouth shut whenever he came to games.

Sometimes I didn't know which was worse, a parent who was up your back or a parent who wished you wouldn't play so much, like my mom.

When the bell rang, I overheard Anna ask Lindsay what Chris Hanson was really like, and I had to smile at Lindsay's answer.

"Beyond gorgeous," she said, "but you have to take a number and get in line. Believe me, that line goes out the door because girls have been waiting forever to have him check them out. It won't do any of them any good, though. Mr. Hanson won't let him think of anything that would interfere with basketball and school."

Now, I had been over to the Hanson house more than any other girl, and I'd known Chris since he was maybe thirteen. As I walked out of the cafeteria, I realized I felt a little bad for Chris because I knew what Lindsay said was right on the money.

I was sitting in algebra, copying down problems from the board, and thinking about Chris Hanson and basketball, and Jules, and her plans for playing hockey in college. I didn't get how she could think of things like that. It was so far off. I mean, we'd just gotten to ninth grade. I couldn't imagine what next week would be like. Suddenly, writing some math problems down in my notebook seemed way less challenging than thinking about the future.

After school, while we were all waiting around in the locker room to get our uniforms, Ms. O'Donnell had us pick numbers out of a hat. She wanted to make it fair for who got to go first and get the best choices. I drew number ten, which could be a good omen for me since that was the uniform number I really wanted. Then I saw Sam walking away from the room, carrying **my** number ten uniform shirts! I felt a growl building in the back of my throat and sent her some evil looks. *I bet she somehow knew that was my number and just took it to spite me.*

When it was my turn, Ms. O'Donnell pointed me to a pile of small kilts and told me to try one on to make sure it fit. I picked out my kilt, I got warm ups in the same size, and Ms. O'Donnell passed me a clipboard.

"What shirt number do you want? Here is the list of numbers left."

"I've always had number ten," I said.

She paused for a minute, then looked up at me. "You know, Sam said the same thing. She just got lucky and got it first. Personally, I think it's always best for players not to pay too much attention to things like what they wear, special charms, or pre-game rituals. Really good players keep it simple: be prepared and focus on the job ahead."

I glanced at her for a moment and slowly looked down at the clipboard. I gave a small smile and looked her in the eyes. "Number two seems okay to me."

She smiled back. "It's as good as any, Jackie."

I hung up my navy and white uniform in my locker, and I thought that Ms. O'Donnell was really cool about the whole thing. I got worked up for nothing. I just wished it hadn't been Sam who had gotten my old number. The most important thing was that I was finally going to be wearing Viking blue and white.

At the end of practice, after we had all done our stretches, we talked about making a pre-game warm up tape, always a big deal for most of the players. Jules reminded the team that she hoped everyone was going to try to make it to the soccer game. Everyone started to get pumped up about being together away from the field, like we were something bigger than a random group of kids. With all that energy jumping, we spontaneously put our hands together and shouted, "Team."

-14-

That night, my parents, Lizzie, and I piled into the car. After we left Lizzie at Emily's party and were driving to the school, I asked, "Where's Cheri? I thought she might come with us."

Mom looked over at Dad and said, "Cheri called and said she couldn't make it."

What's up with that? "But this is his first game. Does Matt know?"

"No, he doesn't," she said. "Thank goodness. He has enough to think about." I looked at Dad's face in the rearview mirror and saw his mouth was kind of grim. I was betting that he wasn't too happy about it, either.

When we got to the field, I took a deep breath and said, "The hockey team is going to sit together. It's our first team activity. I'll meet you back here afterward, okay?"

"That's fine," Mom said. "Have fun, honey."

"We'll miss you rooting with us," Dad said, sounding a little sad.

Mr. Guilt took aim at my heart, but Mom came through with a block. "Burke, she's in high school now. She needs to be with the other students."

I turned to go, but not before giving her a silent high five. *Thanks, Mom. Sometimes you **do** get it.*

Ellen, Lindsay, and a few girls from Gibbstown saw me and waved me over to the other end of the bleachers. Before long, there were twenty-two of us hockey players sitting together, chatting away like we hadn't seen each other in years.

Shortly after the game got going, I could tell it was going to be a seesaw, back-and-forth type of game. Both teams had players who could move the ball quickly down the field.

Tori turned to Lindsay and me. "This is a pretty good turnout; everyone showed up but Sam."

"Where **is** Sam?" I asked. I was kind of annoyed that she wasn't there, but to be honest, I was kind of happy she wasn't, too.

Anna, who was sitting in front of us, turned around and said, "I don't think she wanted to come."

"What's her problem?" Tori asked.

Anna shrugged her shoulders. "She's just got a lot going on."

I didn't get it. What could be more important than being with the team? There was something missing about Sam Jones. Anna was not telling us the whole story, but I could understand her reluctance to give us the news on Sam. I knew the twins and I had secrets that we'd never shared with anyone else. Maybe Anna was in the same boat.

The roar of the crowd broke into my thinking and I turned back to the game. Someone from Northfield's defense had sent a long pass down the field, and now Matt was moving full speed onto the ball. He easily dodged the one remaining defender and drilled the ball into the lower left hand corner of the cage. Everyone stood and cheered.

"Your brother is really good," Anna said.

I smiled and remembered about the scout. I looked over to where my parents were sitting and saw them talking to a man wearing an athletic jacket that was definitely not Northfield colors. I couldn't tell if there was a college name on his jacket, but I hoped it was the scout. I had my fingers crossed that he'd seen Matt's goal.

For the next ten minutes, the game went back and forth, and we were totally into the action on the field. Someone said that the game seemed a lot like field hockey. I thought they were probably right, except soccer had off sides and we didn't, which I thought was way cool; I never had to worry about counting defenders as I took off down the field. That was a good thing, too, since math was never my strongest subject.

The crowd got more and more into the game, and I didn't notice the bleachers quickly filling up around us. There was a pause in the action and I heard someone behind me whisper, "Some game, huh, Reds?"

No way, I can't believe it! I felt myself getting warm and it wasn't the night air. I slowly turned around to find Mitch

Kennedy sitting directly behind me along with five other boys.

"Oh, hi," was the only stupid thing I could say.

Lindsay turned to see who I was speaking to, then elbowed Jules, whispering, "The dude from homeroom." I could have killed her right then.

It was Jules' turn to glance over her shoulder. She smiled. "The plot thickens."

"Which one is your brother?" Mitch asked, totally ignoring my friends' comments, which was a relief.

"Number eleven," I said, grateful for having the job of just answering a simple question instead of doing any thinking. I felt like my brain had been beamed up by aliens. To make matters worse, I could feel my heart racing, while the rest of me was kind of numb.

The boy next to Mitch said, "He's really good." *Hmmmm, seems like everyone else on the planet has **their** mental powers intact.*

Finally, I discovered a few brain cells creeping their way back into my head. I said, "A college recruiter is here to see him play tonight."

"He's sure having a good game so far," the boy said.

Mitch turned to the boy and said, "Kurt, this is Jackie. Jackie, Kurt Evans." I smiled, trying to pretend I had some social skills.

Tori, who was sitting on the other side of me, was not missing any of this conversation. She turned and said hi to the boys, then added, "I'm Tori Hanson, and the beautiful look-alike sitting down there in the jean jacket is my sister,

Jules. And this is Lindsay and Ellen." She pointed out the only other hockey players on our row of bleachers.

By now, some of the other girls had caught the action, and Mitch laughed at the sudden interest. He turned to the other boys and said, "Okay, basketball, meet field hockey." He indicated the tall, rugged boy to his right as Kurt, and then he went right down the line. "Bryan, Tom, Will, and Davey."

Davey, a boy with close-cropped blond hair and a gray hooded sweatshirt, stood up and said, "Mitch got the intros a little wrong. Five of these fools chase a ball up and down the court, but I am part of a real sport — wrestling." That remark brought good natured booing from the other guys.

Pretty soon, some of the boys and girls started to talk with each other. After a few minutes, Mitch leaned toward me and asked if I wanted to go and get something to drink.

"Uh," I said. I felt Tori nudging me in the ribs. I glanced at her. She was looking straight ahead, but she mouthed, "Go."

"Uh, okay," I said to Mitch. I turned to Lindsay on the other side of me and said, "I'll be back in a few minutes."

We walked around the back of the bleachers to the refreshment stand, where it was really dark and kind of hard to see. I knew we could have gone along the front of the bleachers where it was well lit, but that would have meant walking in front of Mom's spotlight eyes, and that was **so** not going to happen.

We hadn't gone far when Mitch said, "Watch that hole, Jackie," and reached for my hand. I stepped over the spot in the ground easily enough and started to slip my hand out of his, but he tightened his fingers around mine.

Suddenly I went all tongue tied again. I was completely focused on the warmth of his hand. It felt really weird. *Does he think I'm an invalid or something who needs to have my hand in his to walk?* The thought made me determined to pull my hand out of his. Of course, I pretended to be cool about it by sliding one of my crazy curls behind my ear.

"How'd I do as a social director?" he asked, not reacting to my little trick.

"Pretty good. Tell me more about your friends," I said, calming down a bit and starting to feel more normal.

"Well, Davey lives down the street from me. We met when I moved here this summer. He introduced me to Kurt. The other guys, Will, Tom, and Bryan, are friends of Kurt, who I met at the basketball courts. They have pickup games at the Morrisville Middle School in the summer, so all of us have actually gotten pretty friendly. Davey is a sophomore, but he has always been friends with Kurt through Little League and then American Legion Baseball, so he's pretty cool about hanging out with some of us freshmen sometimes. You don't mind me bringing them along with me to meet some of your friends, do you?"

"No, I think it's great," I said. "The girls on my team probably like it a lot."

"I'm hoping one of them can hit it off with one of your friends." He surprised me by saying that, but before I had time to think about it, we arrived at the refreshment stand and I was telling him what I wanted to drink.

We were sipping our sodas and taking our time getting back to the bleachers when Mitch asked me how I got to the game.

"I came with my parents. They try to get to as many of Matt's games as they can."

"That's cool. My dad likes to see me play when he isn't away."

Just before we got to the end of the bleacher stands, Mitch said something totally unexpected. "So Jackie, how would you feel about going out sometime?"

What? I looked down and could feel my face heating up again. I was relieved we weren't holding hands just then because my palms were getting all sweaty. "Uh, I don't know." I looked up at him. "I don't know what my parents would say." *There, that's a safe answer. Make Mom and Dad an excuse.*

Mitch was quiet for a moment. We walked around to the front of the bleachers and he said, "Maybe if I meet them it'll help."

Snagged. Now what am I going to do?

I searched for my parents at the other end of the stands. My mom was still sitting up at the top of the bleachers, talking to the scout guy. But my dad was coming down the steps, right toward us. *Now what?* I felt cornered. *I better get this over with. It doesn't mean I have to go out with him. Besides, Dad could say no.*

"Looks like you're going to get your chance. Here comes my dad now," I said.

My dad had his eyes on the game as he was walking. I called out to him and he turned to me with a smile. Then he saw Mitch. He gave him one of those dad stares that only softened a little bit when I introduced Mitch.

Dad reached out to shake Mitch's outstretched hand. Mitch said, "Pleased to meet you, sir."

"So, what position do you play on the hockey team, Mitch?" Dad asked.

"Dad," I hissed between my clenched teeth, "Mitch is in my history class!" *Is this turning into a nightmare or what?*

"Oh, I see," Dad said and actually winked at Mitch.

"He's here at the game with some of his friends," I said nervously. I couldn't believe that my dad had actually winked at a boy I hardly knew.

Mitch picked up the pace of the conversation. "Actually, sir, I wanted to meet you and make sure it was okay if Jackie and I went to the movies sometime."

Now Dad turned all business. "Do you drive?"

"No, sir, I'm just fifteen, I'm a freshman, but I think my father could drive us."

I sensed my dad relax a little. "I guess that would be all right."

Okay, this is enough. My life is spinning out of control. "Dad, we have to get back and watch the game."

We turned to go back to join the friends whose names I suddenly couldn't remember, but Mitch turned to my dad and said, "I'll see you, Mr. McKendry."

I looked back at Dad and he had one of those "man of the house, I'm in charge" kinds of faces on.

As we were climbing the bleachers, I noticed several of my teammates and Mitch's friends had switched seats. Everyone seemed to be getting along, so Mitch and I sat down next to each other.

"Where have you guys been?" Lindsay asked.

"We were talking to my dad," I said. "What's the score?"

"It's still 1-0. Matt's had some good chances, but they have two guys on him now."

Just then, there was an interception of a defense pass by Matt, and he sprinted toward the cage with the ball. As the goalkeeper came out to cut down his angle, Matt slipped the ball to his right and his Northfield teammate stepped up and drilled the ball into the cage. The fans went wild. I turned and high-fived Lindsay, and Mitch put his arm around my shoulders and gave me a quick hug. "That was terrific," he said as he took his arm slowly away.

I smiled up at him and said, "I am so excited for Matt. He's worked so hard. He deserves this."

With the last minute running down on the clock, Mitch started to get up and said, "I think we're going to be heading out, Jackie. I'll see you Monday."

"Okay, see you," I said and gave him a little wave.

As soon as the boys left, all the girls on the team began to slide closer together. It was like somebody pushed a button and everyone started jabbering at once. Finally, Sarah, from Morrisville, came over to me and said, "Jackie, your boyfriend really got the ball rolling, bringing those guys to the game."

"He's not my boyfriend," I said. I was ticked that she even assumed that.

"Well, whatever, he did good," Sarah laughed.

Tori turned to me and whispered, "Seriously, Jackie, I think he's really into you. Do you think he just brought those guys to meet us? It was all about meeting up with you, dummy."

"You think?"

"I know," said Tori.

Soon we were all saying goodbye to one another, and as we drifted away, I thought it was a great idea for us to be together tonight. It was like we had our own special energy together in the stands. I hoped it could bring us together on the field.

My parents were still talking to the scout after the game. They introduced me, and then the scout left to talk with Matt. In the car, my mom couldn't stop talking about the guy. It looked like she was getting into this recruiting thing.

"I think Vermont is really interested in Matt." She turned to me in the back seat. "Their assistant coach worked a soccer camp that Matt attended last summer. I think that's how they learned about him."

"Vermont is really far away," I said, and the reality of my brother being somewhere else next year hit me.

"You're right," Dad said, "but there are other schools coming to see him too. After the season is over, we'll have to visit more college campuses." Even as Dad said this, I was picturing a giant crane reaching out, picking up my brother, and dropping him on a gigantic map of the United States nowhere near New Jersey. The idea left me cold.

We were a few blocks from picking up Lizzie when Dad said, "So Jackie, what's the story on this Mitch?"

"Is he the boy who called the other night?" Mom asked.

I slumped down in my seat. *Here comes the third degree. Might as well fill them in or there will be no end to it.*

"Mitch is in my class at school. You'll be happy to know he's really smart and he's from Texas."

"What is he doing in New Jersey?" Dad asked.

"His father's stationed at McGuire. He's in the military."

"Well, that explains all of the 'yes sirs,' I expect."

"So, it's okay if we go out?" I asked, just in case.

"I suppose," Dad said as he gave me a long look in the rearview mirror. My dad didn't say a lot, but Matt and I knew that our dad was really a shark swimming just below the surface of the water when it came to smelling out anything about us kids. I knew I would never be able to pull a duck and weave on my dad, not ever.

-15-

The next afternoon, I was walking by Matt's room and noticed my brother deep in conversation on the phone. I wondered if he was talking to Cheri. Later on, when we were all sitting around the table after dinner talking about soccer and college, Matt suddenly exploded out of his chair, telling us he was going out.

"Girlfriend trouble?" Dad asked, looking at Mom for confirmation.

"I wouldn't be surprised," Mom said. "I'm not sure how he will react if they break up. I think she's the first girl he's been serious about, but something tells me she has had a string of boyfriends."

"All we can do is give him our support," Dad said.

Lizzie and I cleared the table and stacked the dishes, and I went up to our bedroom. I was sitting at my desk, sorting out homework assignments that I needed to deal with, and while I was going through the loose papers, I started thinking about Mitch Kennedy. I couldn't hide it; I was attracted to him.

When I thought about the last few days, I realized I had actually been looking forward to the times in the day when I saw him at school. I was even checking the hallways when I went from class to class to see if I could spot him, and I did like talking to him 'cause he really got the sports thing.

I thought it would be kind of nice to have a guy friend, someone you could joke around with, and maybe that could happen for Mitch and me. But there was a line between having a friend who happened to be a boy and other things. It was a line I didn't think I wanted to cross.

I tried to imagine what the other side of the line might be like. If Mitch and I were together, not that it would ever happen, I wondered if he would ever make me sad or leave me crying. He seemed nice, but maybe he would start liking another girl instead of me, maybe someone more sophisticated. I might just be some filler 'til basketball started. Who knew?

I thought that maybe I should just say no to going out. I mean, why start something? I thought again of Matt and Cheri. My brother was a mess right now, and it was way worse than a few tears at a dance.

Later, I went downstairs and found Mom in the laundry room, sorting clothes. "Mom, can I ask you a question?"

"Sure, honey."

"If you really like somebody, is it worth it if you wind up being unhappy?"

"Oh, Jackie, that is such a tough question. Are you thinking about Matt and Cheri?"

"Sort of," I said.

"When Matt and Cheri met this summer, it all happened so quickly. He changed so many things in his life for her. The only thing he really held on to was his soccer. You and your brother are different people, Jackie. You're so sensitive it takes you awhile before you can put your trust in someone. And that is not necessarily a bad quality to have." She paused a moment, looked away, and then she said, "If you take your time with someone and get to know them gradually, then you'll make good choices and have a better chance of having happy outcomes.

"But you've got to realize something, Jackie; there are no guarantees in life about not having pain. The way I see it, if you are honest and remain true to yourself, some risks make life worthwhile. Does that help you at all, honey?"

"I think so," I said, wrapping my arm around her waist. For once, my mom had given me some ideas to really think about.

On my way back upstairs, I heard Matt drive up and his car door slam. A moment later, he came up the stairs two at a time, as if he couldn't wait to get to his room and shut out the world. A few moments later, his music was cranked up at full volume.

I was in bed when I heard Dad knock on his door, and then the music was turned down. I could hear the muffled sound of voices, but I couldn't make out what was being said. I wasn't even sure I wanted to know. I buried my head under the pillow and fell asleep.

On Sunday night, Tori called. "Hey Jackie, your boy is the bomb. Davey Barr called me last night and we talked for over an hour."

"I'm glad." *Score another one for my girl, Tori.*

"I found out he's in my lunch, so we hope to see each other tomorrow. Can't talk right now, Jules is calling, got to go; we have to finish the CD. Just wanted to let you know."

I hung up, wondering how it was that these boy things were so easy for Tori. She just seemed to plunge straight ahead while I struggled with the simplest stuff.

-16-

I was still fantasizing about a possible romantic future or a lack of one on the ride to school on Monday. I had to be honest; Mitch Kennedy was more than just some random boy in my class, someone fun to talk to. Should I put a lid on my feelings and just have him as a buddy? I wasn't sure. It felt like a wrestling match going on inside my head. One answer would have the upper hand, and then it would reverse, and the other answer took control.

On my way to homeroom, I started having the same butterflies in my stomach that I got right before the start of a game. *Calm down, girl. At least try to pretend to be cool. Remember what Matt is going through right now.*

As I walked down the aisle to my seat in homeroom, I saw Mitch sitting behind my empty chair. His foot tapping a mile a minute like he was waiting for something.

"Hi Jackie," he said, kind of happy like. "What did your brother think about the scout at the game?"

"Oh, he thought it was okay, I guess. He doesn't talk about it much." I couldn't say that my brother was so devastated about his girlfriend that playing college soccer was probably the last thing on his mind.

Mitch seemed puzzled by my answer but said, "Probably wants to see what's out there first."

I smiled. "Yeah, I guess." *Okay, I'm on top of it. I'm just being regular, buddy to buddy.* I felt a lot better as our conversation continued all casual like, but I knew deep down that my emotions were bouncing around, just waiting to pop out.

At lunch, Jules turned to me. "I think my sister is in love after only twenty-four hours."

"What's up?" Lindsay asked as she joined us.

"One of the boys from the soccer game called Tori," Jules said.

Alisha called out over the conversation, "No more boy talk. I have something serious to discuss. I am planning to run for class president, and I want your help."

This was big news. Quickly, all the usual thoughts of hockey and boys faded away.

"You can count on us," Jules said. "Tell us what you want us to do."

"I think I'm okay with everyone from Washington Elementary. They've known me forever. Besides, Pete Baker is not running for class president again; he already told me. But that leaves me as an unknown to two thirds of the freshman class. I need to get my name and reputation out there to the others. Also, nobody cared about the color of my skin at our old school, but I'm not sure about here. There are probably not more than forty African-American students in this whole high school."

"I never even thought of that," I said, amazed. "I mean, sure, our school is mostly white, but I didn't think it was a big deal."

Alisha turned to me and said, "You wouldn't." She hesitated and then said, "That's not a put down, Jackie. If the positions were reversed, I would probably say the same thing."

"Maybe it won't matter in the voting," I said.

"Maybe," said Alisha. "We'll see."

I felt embarrassed. I shouldn't have said anything at all. We didn't usually bring up race; it was an uncool thing to do. I didn't know why I said anything. It just kind of slipped out. Looking down at my suddenly unappetizing pizza, I wanted to disappear, or at least start the whole conversation over.

Jules saved my awkward silence when she said enthusiastically, "Alisha, give us your platform for the class and then we'll start telling others."

"Kerry and I would like to help too," Anna said. "We know lots of people from Morrisville."

"Thanks, guys," Alisha said. "You're the best."

As we were leaving the lunchroom, Alisha touched my arm and I stopped. She looked at me. "Jackie, don't sweat it, okay?" I smiled back. I hope she meant it and wasn't only trying to be nice.

I was still thinking about Alisha's comment when I got to my next class. I never thought the fact that Alisha was black made her different. She was just Alisha. Even reading my book for English about the life of Jane Pitman didn't seem to have any connection to today and the girl who had always been a leader in our class.

It made me think. What was it like to be one of the few minority students in a school? Was school really different for them? It was a pretty hard thing to imagine. As I slid into my seat and opened up my math book, I wondered if I was the only one at the table who took Alisha's acceptance by everyone for granted. *And*, I thought, *why do we never talk about stuff like that?*

After world history, Mitch walked me to the gym. "Davey made a move on your friend Tori. He said he likes a girl who's playful and confident."

I looked up at him, grinning. "That's Tori for sure, but she's great, too."

"Then maybe we can all go out together next week. What do you think?"

Ladies and gentlemen, it's the third round of the match and neither wrestler has the advantage. They are facing each other straight up. What do I want to do? I couldn't use my parents as an excuse anymore. I felt like I was being pulled in half. My nerves won out. I said, "I don't think so."

He looked a little sad, but he slid past the awkwardness and said, "Oh, okay. Maybe some other time."

I may have been tying on my cleats in the locker room, but I was thinking about having said no to the date with Mitch, wondering if I had been stupid. Maybe he wouldn't even speak to me anymore, or maybe he would go ask some other girl out. To be honest, I didn't like that idea one bit. Then I realized I was thinking way too much and I was going to be late for practice.

At dinner that night, things were very quiet. Matt kept his eyes down the whole time and Dad seemed tense. I couldn't take it anymore and broke the silence. "Matt, I thought you played great Friday night. Did you hear us cheering?"

"Yeah," he mumbled. "It was a good turnout; the guys were pumped." He might have been saying all the right words, but they sure sounded empty to me. I looked at his eyes, and it seemed to me like somebody needed to put out a report on a missing heart.

"So, when's your next game?" I asked, trying to perk him up a little.

"We play Wednesday at Waretown and Saturday at Eisenhower," he said without feeling, then turned to our dad and asked to be excused. He didn't even wait for Dad's answer but stood up, pushed in his chair and went to his room.

"I need to speak to him," Mom said.

"Give him some space, Anne."

"So it's over?" I asked.

"Yes, dear, it is," Mom said.

"What's over?" asked Lizzie, suddenly curious.

"Summer, summer's over, Lizzie," I answered as I got up to clear the dishes.

-17-

I woke up with a smile the next morning because this was game day. Lying in bed, I could feel the adrenaline rush just thinking about it. About the time I finished dressing, there was a knock on my door. It was Matt.

"If you want, I'll drive you to school."

"Thanks, that'll be great," I said, my already good mood turning up a notch. I mean, it'd be fantastic to start the day being driven to school and not riding the old number eighty-six bus. But then I realized I was probably a poor substitute for Cheri, and that kind of sobered me up a bit.

After breakfast, I hopped into the car with my brother. He popped in a CD, and off we rode into the world of alternative music. Let me tell you, if I could listen to music when I was on the hockey field, there would be no stopping me. I might be a tomboy, but I love my rhythms.

When we were young, the twins and I used to go to their room and stand on top of their beds where we could see ourselves in the mirror and pretend we were dancers on MTV. Even their brother, Chris, was not spared our shenanigans. At first he balked, but the twins were mighty persistent when they wanted something, and before long there were four of us dancing like we were backups for some rappers.

Matt turned down the volume as we pulled into the student parking lot. Once we'd parked, I thanked him for the ride, but before I got out of the car I said, "I realize I'm just a little punk of a sister, but I want you to know that I'm sorry you and Cheri didn't work out. I think you're the best big brother a girl could have." And I meant it; Matt had always been there for me when we were growing up, always on the lookout, making sure I was okay.

"Thanks, kiddo," he said, giving my arm a squeeze. As we got out of the car, he looked over the roof and said, "Make them know a McKendry is on the field today, Jackie."

The day seemed to fly by, and before I knew it, I was in the locker room getting dressed for the game. I looked in the mirror. *This is it, my first game as a high school player.* I took a second glance at my hair. Tori had taught me how to pull up the sides of my hair to the top of my head with a band to keep it from falling in my face. It did look decent, but I sure missed my old ponytail.

Ellen came up behind me and playfully pushed me away from the mirror. "Hey, Jackie, if you look at yourself any longer you'll miss the whole first half."

I laughed. "Yeah, I should just turn around and check out what the other team is going to see when I blow by them."

Ellen put her arm around my shoulders as we walked out the door. "Jackie, you're so much fun. I'm glad we're friends." I smiled back at her and thought, *This is going to be a good afternoon.*

The warm up CD the twins made for the team was awesome. It had all the girls pumped up. As we were going through the drills, I took a moment to look around the field at my teammates working hard in their navy and white uniforms. Then I glanced at the opposite end of the field and saw the other team warming up in their orange and brown.

I love it, the colors, the crack of sticks hitting balls. The best part is my friends being with me, everyone waiting for the game to start. This is the greatest thing in the whole world.

Ms. O'Donnell called us in. "You may have noticed I have not named captains. There are so many potential leaders among you that I would like everyone to have an opportunity to be a captain for a while. I think it will give all of you an appreciation for what it takes to lead a team and what a challenge it can be. How does everyone feel about that?"

The team seemed to like her idea, so she went on and said, "Today I'm asking Jules Hanson and Heather Whitcraft to act as captains for the coin toss." Then she read out the starting lineup. It was similar to the last scrimmage, but I knew that some positions were still not settled. Kerry was still starting in goal, but I hoped that Ms. O'Donnell would give Becky a chance to play too.

Near the end of the first half, I slipped the ball around the goalkeeper on Jules' penalty corner shot, making the score 1-0 at the half. In the second half, I dribbled the ball down the left side of the field and at the last minute pushed the ball over to Sam for an easy goal. There wasn't much action for Kerry, and in the last ten minutes, our coach put in Becky.

While Becky only had one save, it was good to have her back on the field. I thought the defense stepped up a notch when Becky was back there directing them. The final goal of the game was a penalty stroke, which was taken by Jules. Although the team was pumped up with this first win, I felt like we weren't really challenged. I thought things were going to get tougher, and I sure hoped we'd be ready.

That night Mitch called, which surprised me, but in a happy way. Maybe his calling meant we could still be friends and he wasn't mad or anything.

"Are you giving out autographs, Reds?"

"What do you mean?"

"I was at the game with Kurt and Davey."

"I didn't even see you."

"We'd been in the gym playing ball, and we didn't get there until just before your goal. The team looks pretty good. Your brother has nothing on you, though. I think I'm talking to the number one athlete in the McKendry house."

I wondered how he felt about that. I knew it was one thing for a girl to say she was on a team, walking around in the school colors, but it was way different to be known as a serious athlete. It made some guys freak. If Mitch was like that, it would pretty much end our friendship or whatever was going on real quick.

"It looks like you're into hockey like I'm into basketball," he said. "That's cool."

I smiled, relieved. I could be a jock and his friend at the same time, and he was okay with it. I just didn't know for sure if that was all I wanted.

-18-

On Wednesday, I got my first English paper back. It was on the Ernest Gaines book. I had put in a lot of time on it 'cause I thought a lot of the story. How could you read about all that struggle and courage and not try to write a good paper? After I finished it, I remembered reading it and rereading it to get it just right.

I looked at what the teacher had written. He had scrawled on the paper, "Well done, you show promise," with a B+ written below. I was a little disappointed until I saw some of the other kids' shocked faces with grades of C's and D's. *It's a good thing I put the time in. Maybe I **can** become a good student.*

At lunch, Alisha laid out the plan for her campaign. It was really clever and included lots of good points that I thought the freshman class could get into. Lindsay suggested that we make flyers and pass them out, but Alicia said we couldn't do anything official until Monday. Jules volunteered Tori for the flyers, which was a good idea 'cause Tori was super creative on the computer.

"We'll have three days to campaign with an assembly on Wednesday," Alisha said. "On Thursday, people vote in homeroom. They'll also elect a homeroom representative to student council. On Friday, everyone will know the results."

Listening to all this strategy, I said, "This is like a mini hockey season. Prepare, play, and get a win." Alisha rolled her eyes because I was always thinking like everything in life related to sports. I just couldn't help it.

That night, my mom and dad were going to Matt's away game and would be getting home late. Mom left a meal for Lizzie and me, and after we cleaned up, I was pretty surprised by how easy it was for me to get into my homework routine. What amazed me most was that it was a boy's attitude about school that got me going in the right direction.

Before I went to bed, I heard my parents' car and I went downstairs to show them my paper and find out about Matt's game. My parents were already sitting at the table when I walked into the kitchen.

"Hey, did Matt's team win?"

Mom looked up and smiled at me. "Yes, barely. 1-0."

"How did Matt do?"

"He had a tough night," Dad said. "It was a shame; there was a coach from Long Island University at the game, but he left by halftime."

Mom pounded the table with her fist, making me jump. I was shocked; that was **so** not like my mom.

"It's all that Cheri's fault," she said with a heat I'd never heard from her before. "He is moping around over someone who is simply not worth it."

Dad looked at Mom, then to me. "Jackie, you really should get to bed."

"Oh, here," I said, pushing the paper across the table to Dad. "I got a good grade on my English paper."

As I turned to go, Mom reached out for my arm. "I'm sorry, Jackie. I shouldn't be so upset. I'm glad you did well on your paper."

"Mom, there are a million girls at Northfield who would die to go out with Matt. You should see the girls in the hallways checking him out when he walks by with his friends. Besides, he's such a good person."

"Yes, he is, just right now a sad one," Mom said.

I headed upstairs, thinking that parents can really surprise you sometimes. My mom was really hot just then. Now, if she was an athlete, not that I think she ever was, more like a homecoming queen, she could seriously take some people out. *Good for you, Mom*, I thought. *I'd like to bury Cheri myself right about now.*

Lying in bed, I thought this week had sure been all over the place. Alisha was running for president, I said no to Mitch, and I had my first high school game. Crazy!

Then my mind drifted to my brother and his love for soccer. He felt about soccer just like I felt about hockey. I turned over to flip off the light, and I made up my mind that if I could help him get back into his game, I would.

Matt offered to drive me to school the next day, and while we were riding, I reached out and turned down the music. "Matt, can we talk?"

"Sure, Jack," he said, and glanced my way.

That gave me some courage so I asked, "How long have you been playing soccer?"

He looked at me, wondering where I was going with the question. "I guess since I was seven or eight."

"So for ten or more years, you have put a lot of time in on something you really love. And how long were you and Cheri together?"

Matt was silent for a minute. "Maybe three months."

"Do the math, Matt."

Matt's hands gripped the wheel tighter. "Jackie, you don't understand."

"No, I probably don't. I know you were crazy about her. You guys were together every day this summer at the swim club, and it was easy for you to be a couple. Now she is back in her own school with her own friends. She's only a junior; she's not even thinking about college. You can be ticked off at me for saying all this, but I think you should just think about something that you have always counted on — soccer. There, I'm done."

Matt didn't say anything; he just cranked up the volume on the stereo, looked straight ahead, and drove. When we got to school, he got out of the car, slammed the door, and walked away without saying a word to me. I stood by the car for a moment. *What have I done? I had no business putting my two cents in. What do I know, anyway?*

In homeroom, Mitch said, "Jackie, you look kind of bummed. What's up?"

"I was talking to my brother this morning and I said some things I probably shouldn't have, and now he's ticked off at me."

"He'll get over it. How could anybody stay mad at you? You're too cute." I smiled. I did appreciate Mitch's attempt to make me feel better, but I was beginning to think I should have just left Matt alone.

The afternoon's game was away at New Gretna, and when the team got off the bus, Ms. O'Donnell pulled Steph Jankowski and me aside and told us we would act as captains for the day.

Steph and I let the others walk ahead of us so we could discuss the captain stuff.

"Jackie, I'm not much of a talker. What should we say?"

I was thinking, *Just heads or tails. That'll be pretty much it for me.* But I knew she didn't want some wiseacre comment. "I don't know. Maybe we should get everyone talking on defense — you know, who has ball, stuff like that. Coach is always saying it's important. Besides that, I just think we should keep people pumped up and work hard. Then, if they see us really pushing it out there, maybe that will be good enough."

"Works for me, Jackie," Steph said, sounding relieved.

The game started out with us really pressing New Gretna's defense. We were getting pretty confident that scoring was going to be easy, just like the last game, but it turned out that their goalkeeper was tough. After awhile, we started getting frustrated 'cause we couldn't finish any of our plays with a goal.

We got desperate and sloppy and started hitting long, hard passes toward the goal that the other team easily intercepted. At the half, Ms. O'Donnell made one sub, Becky for Kerry, but nothing our coach said or did at halftime seemed to make a difference to the team. We were self-destructing right before our eyes.

Steph and I tried to cheer the team on, and we both worked as hard as we could, but the team was even more sluggish as we moved through the second half. Finally, in frustration, Ms. O'Donnell subbed in all new players with ten minutes left. Only the outstanding stops and clears by Becky kept the other team from scoring. At the end of the game, Becky had twelve saves, and the game ended 0-0.

After the game, Ms. O'Donnell talked to the team. "We started out strong as a team, but when things did not go our way and we didn't score, we started to not believe in ourselves. That's when we put on 'doubting shoes.' You know, those shoes that say, 'I doubt that I can do the job, I doubt that you can do the job, and I doubt that we can do the job together."

She gave us a moment to let it sink in, then said, "We are much more aware of each other and much more improved in our teamwork than we were a week ago, and that's good. But what we need to figure out is when things don't go our way, how deep can we dig down and make things turn around for us? In other words, we need to learn how to throw away those doubting shoes forever."

She eyeballed each one of us like she was trying to push those words straight into our brains. I knew right then that becoming a great team was a lot more complicated than I thought, and we had a long way to go.

Dinner that night was quiet. It seemed to me like I was sitting all by myself in an empty room. Matt was home but he wasn't saying much, and even Lizzie wasn't her usual bubbly self. Finally, Dad broke the silence.

"So Jackie, did you have a game today?"

"Yeah, Dad. We tied 0-0. They had a good goalkeeper, but we should have won. We got down on ourselves and couldn't make it better."

"I'm sorry," Dad said. "That can happen to a lot of teams, and to players, too. I know you and the girls will figure things out, though." He smiled at me like he really believed we could do it. He was looking at me when he said it, but I think he was including Matt in that smile.

The next day's ride to school was as quiet as last night's dinner until we turned into the parking lot. Still looking straight ahead, Matt said, "Who's this Mitch character who keeps calling you?"

"He's in my homeroom. He plays basketball."

"Did he go to Washington last year?"

"No, he's from Texas. He and his dad moved here this summer."

Matt's face was set and he didn't really say anything else, just goodbye when we got out of the car. As I walked into the building, I was hoping that the deep freeze between Matt and me was melting and I could have my old brother back.

At lunch, an older girl, who was athletic-looking and had light sandy hair that reached halfway down her back, came up to our table. She looked right at me and asked if I was Matt McKendry's sister. The table got all quiet around me.

I nodded, and she said, "Hi, I'm Maggie Brooks. I'm in Matt's class. I saw you both coming into school today, and I was wondering…is Matt still going with that girl from East Morris? I know he had been driving her to school."

I was stunned. I mean, even if I had been offered a hundred dollars to guess what this girl was going to say when she came up to us, I would have had to have taken a pass. I really didn't know how much to tell this girl. I wasn't big on coughing up information for no good reason, so I kind of hedged my answer.

"Well, I can tell you he's been driving me the last couple of days. If you want to know more, I'd ask him if I were you."

The girl's eyes brightened. I thought this might have been the answer she was hoping to hear when she said, "Thanks, maybe I will," and walked away.

Lindsay looked at me. "What was that all about?"

"I think my brother might have a secret admirer." *And maybe I just helped old Cupid out.*

On Sunday afternoon, Mom asked if I would like to go to the mall with her. "The weather is getting cooler, and I think you need a few things. Let's go through your closet."

Normally, I would have passed on the whole shopping thing and just let my mom pick stuff out for me. I'd never really cared that much about fashion, especially my mom's ideas about fashion, but now I thought I should probably look a little better for my classes.

As we went through the junior department, I was feeling overwhelmed by the choices. Girly-girl was definitely out, but there was probably something more than plain jeans and sweats I could wear. But what?

"Mom, help, I need some ideas!"

Those words were like a carrot for a horse. I could see the gleam in my mom's eyes. She'd probably been waiting for me to say those magic words for years.

"How about some dress jeans, dark washed ones. A couple of sweaters would be good, too. Ready to try a miniskirt?" she asked hopefully.

I wasn't sure about the last one, but I liked her other ideas.

"Mom, I also want some boots. You know, something to make me look a little taller."

"And why would you want that?" my mom laughed, and I playfully answered her by making a face and sticking out my tongue.

We settled on a pair of chocolate jeans that fit me perfectly and a brown sweater. Then we added an off-white bulky sweater to our purchases. I really liked its high rolled collar. It was fairly heavy, but cut so I didn't feel like a little peanut in it.

Mom insisted on one nice outfit. When I asked what for, she looked kind of vague and said, "Well, for holidays, things like that."

It seemed like we tried on everything in the store, and I was getting tired and kind of cranky. I needed a food intervention! But my mom was on a roll and wouldn't stop.

She finally coaxed me into a dark olive mini dress. I'll admit it showed off what all the training had done for my legs. It was a jersey knit with a round neck, fitted sleeves, and a high waist. I stood in front of the mirror in the changing room, just checking things out. Then I got a little carried away and busted some moves on my mom like I was on some dance show. She cracked up. We did have our moments, and for once, I felt like I looked special.

We found some matching tights and then hunted for some shoes and boots. It had been a good afternoon. Our shopping done, we wandered around the mall for a while and she bought me some ice cream. I think it was like a pat on the head for being a good girl, you know, like when your parents promise you a treat after a trip to the dentist.

Before we left, my mom tried to nudge me toward a cosmetics counter, but I told her she'd used up her ticket and the train was leaving the station. You couldn't give in to a parent twice in one day — it'd spoil them.

Driving home, I thanked her for the clothes and for being such a big help.

"Jackie, you will never know how much I enjoyed this until you have your own daughter someday," she replied.

I figured that was one of those comments a daughter held on to for a long time.

-19-

In homeroom, I was looking over one of the circulars Tori had designed for Alisha's campaign when Mitch leaned over my shoulder.

"What's this?"

"Our friend, Alisha Wahler, is running for president. She's a great person, super organized, and a really hard worker."

"Good thing to know."

"Would you be willing to give out some of these circulars to the people in your classes?"

"Sure, no problem. I'll let people know what you said, too."

The day was filled with slogans, promises, and campaign workers trying to get votes for their candidates. I was curious to hear what all the candidates were going to say in their assembly speeches on Wednesday, and I wondered how much it would influence the voting. I hadn't seen the whole slate of freshmen who were running, but Alisha had told us something about a couple of people who weren't from Washington Elementary.

The hallways were plastered with campaign posters. A lot of work had gone into some of them. I thought Alisha's were great; they were simple, snappy, and to the point. Then I spotted a poster that surprised me. Emma Connors was running for class secretary. *Well, I'm one vote Emma is **not** going to get.*

See, I've always looked at Emma as a big phony. I knew for a fact that Emma would pretend to be interested in a person and be their friend, and then she'd turn right around and talk about that person behind their back. Several times when we were younger, I saw Emma use people to get what she wanted or until something better came along. I sure wasn't perfect, but I just didn't have time for people like that. There had to be a better candidate for class secretary than her.

At practice, Ms. O'Donnell had a surprise for us. She told us that since the varsity was practicing in the gym to prepare for a turf game, we were getting a chance to scrimmage the junior varsity. Everyone was excited and couldn't wait to play on the varsity field, which was smooth and fast, not like our bumpy field. We also knew we needed to fix our game after that horrible 0-0 tie. The scrimmage would be perfect.

We went through our daily stick work drills and then went to the varsity field. For the lineup, Ms. O'Donnell put in players who normally sub first and had us starters watch for a few minutes. The junior varsity only had a few shots and barely dominated our subs. We cheered the subs on, and we were really getting into it 'cause they never got much of a chance to show what they could do. Then Ms. O'Donnell put us starters on the field.

I could tell the junior varsity thought playing us freshmen was a joke. They were all laughing among themselves and fooling around. It seemed like a real put down to me, as if we were big nothings. But we started to show them otherwise when our defenders began cutting off the JV's casual passes and the momentum started going our way.

I took a quick shot on cage, and Sam was there for the goalkeeper's rebound and slammed it home. I loved that sound. She was surprised when I ran up to her and gave her a high five. Sometimes you just had to overlook a person's obnoxious behavior when you're fired up.

"Game on," Jules said to me under her breath as I ran back to the center line to restart play. The intensity began to pick up on both sides, and play started getting very physical.

At the half, the score was still 1-0. Ms. O'Donnell told us she was going to put the subs in again, but the subs saw how things were shaping up and said, "No, leave them in. We want to see what happens."

The second half was the most intense half I had ever played. A JV player going after a loose ball tried to run through Jules. *Big mistake, girl.* I almost laughed out loud when the girl bounced off of Jules like she had just hit a brick wall and landed on the ground. Sam could be "mean" tough, but Jules was just tough.

As the minutes wound down, Heather Whitcraft picked up a loose ball off of Kerry's clear and started dribbling out of the defensive end of the field. She sent a long pass down the sideline to Steph, who took off, leaving her defender in the dust.

Just as the ball was about to go out of bounds over the end line, Steph saved it and sent a flat pass across the mouth of the goal. I sprinted like crazy and caught up to the pass at the last minute. I barely touched the ball with a reverse stick move, and the ball went flying into the goal cage.

As the players ran back to the center line to restart play again, one of the defenders from the JV turned to me and said in a nasty tone, "You were **so** lucky."

I almost stumbled as I jogged back to the center. Was it luck? Why was she being so mean? I could feel tears come to my eyes, but I blinked them away and tried to put her comments out of my mind.

On the whistle, the JV took possession of the ball and started moving down the field toward Kerry. Anna missed a tackle, making Lindsay the only defender left. As two JV attackers came toward her, Lindsay tried to get to the ball, but one of the junior varsity attackers held Lindsay out so she couldn't make a play for the ball. The JV got into the striking circle, shot, and scored. When the whistle blew, the final score stood at 2-1.

The JV coach came up and thanked Ms. O'Donnell for the good competition, but several JV players made comments to our team as we jogged off the field.

"Don't think you're all that good, because you're not."

"Girl," one of them called out to Jules, "knocking Peyton down was not a good idea."

The comments stunned us, but we didn't want to whine about anything to Ms. O'Donnell. Instead, we huddled together and gave a cheer.

We were still talking about the scrimmage while we waited for the buses, and Heather said, "They were jerks."

"I can't believe they were so nasty about a little scrimmage," another player said.

The whole conversation made me feel a little better about the defender's comment. I really needed to have a thicker skin. I was just so surprised by the JV's attitude. I might have expected stuff like that when we played another school, but not from a team from our own school. *No wonder Britt had complained about the upperclassmen and their attitudes.*

Mitch called again that night. I was kind of getting used to his phoning, and I actually looked forward to our nighttime talks. He made it easy 'cause he seemed genuinely interested in my day and what I was doing. It was like having a friend, but not, at least on my end. It was far more exciting.

-20-

By Tuesday, the freshman campaigns were cranked up a notch, and by Wednesday morning, everyone was pumped for the assembly. As we walked out of homeroom, Mitch looked like he was starting to reach out for my hand, but he just touched my arm and said, "Let's sit together."

I looked down at his hand and wondered what it would be like to have his hand in mine, something the whole school could see.

"So, who do you think you'll vote for?" he asked as we continued to move through the crowded hallway toward the auditorium.

"I'm not sure. I want to hear them speak first before I decide."

While we were walking, it struck me how Mitch made it seem like walking with me was no big deal, like we were good friends, and I asked myself why I felt a little empty about that.

Just then, an older couple was walking toward us, hand in hand. The boy was looking at the girl like she was the only person in the whole world, and the girl looked pretty much like she was crazy about him, too. We passed each other, and I wondered how a boy and a girl got from where Mitch and I were, which I guessed was friends, to a place like that.

We settled into our auditorium seats and waited for the first candidates to speak. Emma Connors was the first speaker for the office of class secretary. She was dressed to kill in a sophisticated black suit with very high heels. *Who does she think she is — some big shot business executive? Or maybe she's auditioning to be the weather girl on TV. Some of them dress like that.*

Mitch looked over at me. "What's with the face? Do you know her?"

"Yeah, sort of," I said.

"She's kind of hot," he laughed. I couldn't help myself. I just reacted and elbowed him hard in the ribs. I cringed and lowered my head. *I can't believe I just did that. What's the matter with me?*

Mitch doubled over laughing. Then a teacher behind us whispered, "Hush."

Mitch leaned toward me and whispered, "Uh oh, I think I've touched a nerve."

Trying to save face, I turned to him and whispered back, "What are you talking about? I was just stretching."

He covered his face 'cause he could barely control himself and he didn't want us to get into trouble again with the teacher behind us.

I perked up when it was time for the presidential candidates. Alisha looked so comfortable up there. She spoke to our class just like she was talking to us at our lunch table. A couple of the other kids who had spoken earlier acted like they couldn't breathe. I thought one guy was going to pass out. That would be me for sure. Six people in a room would probably be my magic limit, and they would have to be my teammates.

As Alicia talked, I thought about how gutsy she was to speak in front of all the students, knowing that a few might not like her just because of her skin color. I didn't think I could ever do anything as brave as that. I couldn't even say yes to a date with a boy I really liked.

The vote for class officers was on Thursday. I had my fingers crossed for Alisha. I hoped that other students saw her leadership ability and didn't think of her in any other way. We were also voting on class representatives for student council, and Mitch was a unanimous pick. I was excited for him and knew he would do a good job for our homeroom.

By that afternoon, elections and hand holding went skipping out of my mind. We were getting dressed for our home game when a senior hockey player walked up to Jules. Of course, I listened.

"I hear you guys had an interesting scrimmage yesterday."

Jules stared down at the girl. "I guess so."

"Tell all your little teammates that they are invited to a special hockey get-together, a sleepover at my house, at 7:30 on Friday. Bring sleeping bags. Here are the directions." She handed Jules some papers and added, "By the way, all the freshmen are expected to be there, no exceptions. Make sure everyone knows it."

Jules came over to Lindsay and me. "Did you hear that?"

"Sounded a little snotty, if you ask me," Lindsay said.

"Well, maybe that's just her," I said. "Maybe they're having a welcome to Northfield field hockey kind of party." Lindsay and Jules looked at me like I was from outer space. "And maybe she's just having a bad day," I added, despite my friends' looks.

"Right, Jackie," Lindsay said, laughing. "She's probably just PMS-ing." Then she walked out the locker room door, shaking her head like she couldn't believe what came out of my mouth sometimes.

The afternoon's game was really over in the first fifteen minutes as both Tori and I scored on penalty corners. By halftime, the score was 4-0. Ten minutes into the second half with the score at 5-0, Ms. O'Donnell cleared the bench, which was great for the girls who don't get to play much. She was still starting Kerry and then having Becky play the second half, but I thought that strategy wouldn't stay around very long once the league competition started to heat up.

We got the election results in Friday's homeroom. Alisha Wahler was freshman class president, Dylan Brooks was vice president, Emma Connors was secretary, and Adam Zigler was treasurer. I was very happy for Alisha, and my excitement for her outweighed the news that people didn't have the common sense to see through Emma Connors.

Before the bell rang to end the homeroom period, Mitch handed me a note. It said,

Reds—I'm still nursing a bruised rib. But the pain can't compare with what I'll feel if you say no again. Please say yes, you'll go out with me.

Mitch

I looked at it twice. Then I grabbed hold of my cowardly heart and remembered what Mom said about taking risks in life. I turned around in my seat and looked him squarely in the face. It seemed like he was holding his breath, waiting for my answer. I just nodded my head, yes, and watched the sparks light up in his warm, gray eyes. I would not have traded seeing that for anything.

I didn't mention anything about my date at lunch because all the focus was on Alisha and the election results. It was her time to shine. *The Table* decided we would bow down when she got to the table. Our little salute made her laugh at our silliness.

"Forget about me being class president. You girls just made me Queen Cleopatra. That's way better."

We were enjoying the celebration when Britt spoke up. "Yesterday, I heard that you guys are being invited to a hockey party tonight. Is that true?"

Yeah," said Lindsay. "Some girl with a major attitude gave us the directions to her house."

"I don't know for sure what's going on," Britt said. "They're keeping pretty quiet about it, and that makes me suspicious. I don't want to make any trouble, but something doesn't feel right about whatever they're planning. I just wanted to give you a heads up."

"Thanks for warning us. We'll talk to the team," Jules said.

We asked Ms. O'Donnell if we could meet with the team for a few minutes at the end of practice. She said it was okay and started walking back to the gym.

"Some of us have heard rumors that tonight might not be all fun and games," Jules said. "Maybe the rumors are nothing. I don't know."

"Then let's not go," somebody said.

"I think since they said it was required, we would look like cowards if we didn't go," Anna said.

"Maybe they just want to have some fun with us," another girl said, sounding hopeful.

Jules seemed to be taking in everyone's point of view. I thought maybe that was why she was a good leader, but then she surprised me and said, "Our dad told us some stories about what some teams have done to younger players, so maybe we should be prepared for anything." She paused, then added, "Here's what I think we should do...."

-21-

Following Jules' plan, we arrived at the senior's house in groups of threes or fours so no one had to face the upperclassmen alone. The girl who gave Jules the directions greeted us at the door and introduced herself as Carly Benson. She led us downstairs into the recreation room, and within twenty minutes, the room was filled with nine seniors and us twenty-four freshmen. Carly's parents didn't seem to be in the house, and I thought that was kind of weird when you're having people at your house for a sleepover.

One of the freshmen asked, "Where are the other girls? Isn't this party for everyone?"

A senior said, "Oh, they'll be with us later."

The captains, Jill Taylor and Kristina Donaldson, introduced themselves and the other seniors. I recognized one of the girls as Maggie Brooks, the girl who had asked about Matt.

Jill started talking about how that evening was supposed to be some kind of test to see if we were worthy to become part of the Northfield hockey tradition. I didn't like the word "test" and looked at Jules.

The other captain, Kristina, told us to put our sleeping bags in the corner and asked if anyone had cell phones. A weird question; everyone always had their cell phones with them. I thought some of the girls had been born with their phones cemented to their ear since they never seemed to be able to put them down.

Of course, I was the exception. I didn't have a cell phone. Mom and Dad thought I'd misuse it and not focus on what I needed to focus on, which was totally bogus if you asked me. They did promise to get me one for my fifteenth birthday, but that was a long way off.

Anyway, this Kristina went on about the phones, saying that the seniors didn't want anything to happen to them, so they were going to collect them and put them in a corner. We were told to shut them off and put our names on them with some tape.

Maggie Brooks came around to collect the phones. "Sorry," she whispered as she passed by me. It was all starting to get a little creepy, and a lot of my teammates were upset about having to give up their cell phones.

The seniors handed us some oversized white T-shirts and told us to put them on. Kristina started speaking. "We know you freshmen realize your proper place and worship us seniors from your lowly positions, so tonight we are going to give you something to remember us by. We're all going to autograph these shirts with little reminders of what we think of you."

Jules gave me a "whatever" kind of look and winked. I was thinking this was all so dumb. It looked like some sorority initiation that you'd see in a B movie. I never thought sports people would be into stuff like this, but if this was all the seniors were going to do, write some stupid stuff on a shirt, I figured I'd live.

After they finished writing on the front and back of our shirts, we looked at each other's shirts and could see they had written some pretty disgusting things on them.

"I don't think your look is quite complete yet," one of them said.

The next thing we knew, they were putting mousse, gel, and color spray in our hair. We looked totally ridiculous. In a way, I thought it was kind of funny. It was sort of like Halloween. But some of my teammates were very particular about how they looked, and they were not into this at all. Once they had us looking the way they wanted, Kristina pointed her cell phone at us one by one and told us to say our first name and uniform number, "So you'll be immediately recognized by anyone that matters."

I thought that things were getting stranger by the minute with the camera thing, and some of the girls were getting more upset and didn't want their pictures taken. They certainly didn't want anyone to see the pictures.

Ellen and Anna were trying to get the ones who were most upset to chill, but Jill and another senior snapped, "Freshmen, don't speak unless you're spoken to."

When things got quiet, Jill said, "Now, we are going on a little ride. We want it to be a surprise, so all of you will be blindfolded, and then you'll be put into cars. Don't worry. This will be fun. You'll see."

We were all blindfolded and led up the stairs and out onto the lawn.

157

I heard, "No talking," yelled out again and again. Someone bumped into me and I felt her trip and fall down; then I heard weeping. I inched my way down to her. I was thinking it might be Sam, and without saying a word, I lifted her up. I mean, even though I sometimes wanted to stamp on her, these upperclassmen were messing with my teammate. I kept my arm around her and patted her arm, and soon the crying stopped.

I was put into the back seat of a car along with a teammate. I occasionally heard a voice that I recognized as Jill's and a boy's response and a laugh. I didn't know how long we rode, but it was starting to get a little cold without a coat on. I sensed the car leaving the paved road and moving along a rutted path. *Where are they taking us?*

It wasn't long before the car stopped. The other freshman and I were told to get out. We were led for what seemed to be about fifty yards and then told to stand still. I could hear a lot of voices and cheering. I thought my teammates were somewhere around me.

Then it quieted down and one of the seniors said, "You think you're such a great team, and you seem to not mind showing off for people, so we've decided to give you a real audience. Audience, let them know you're here."

Suddenly, we heard clapping and yelling and whistles from what seemed to be dozens of boys and girls. The boys probably felt all brave in front of a bunch of us blindfolded girls 'cause they hurled out comments that I was sure they'd never have dared to say to us face to face.

"It's time you paid for thinking that your team's so great. Since you freshmen are so, so talented, we've decided you're going to entertain us tonight. We want you to dance for us, and we won't take your blindfolds off until you do."

I sensed nobody moving.

"Dance, freshmen, dance!"

It was getting so cold just standing there. I hated this, and I was sure my teammates did too. I wished I could say something or do something; like push a magic button that would whisk us all away, but I knew my pockets were as empty as my head.

Finally, I heard Tori's voice. "Hey guys, remember that song on our warm up CD?" Then she started to hum it. One of the girls started to pick up with the lyrics. Another voice joined in, shaking at first, but then it got stronger. Pretty soon, everyone on the team was joining in.

I sensed the energy growing all around me. The girl next to me, I thought it might be Kerry, started to clap to the music. People were beginning to move, and I got caught up in it. I was thinking this team had more strength inside than we ever thought.

The only sound was our singing. When it ended, a boy from the audience yelled, "Good job, freshmen!" and there was some scattered applause.

Coming over the top of the clapping came the sound of Jill's voice. "Time to leave, everybody." She sounded really annoyed, like this was not exactly the way things were supposed to be going.

I heard the muffled sounds of people picking up things and moving away, and the next thing I heard were the sounds of cars being started.

Jill was still barking orders, trying to scare us, I guess. "Since you all like being together so much, we're going to make sure you stay that way."

Someone started tying each of our left hands to the right hand of one of our teammates. It was done in a way so we couldn't really reach out and get our blindfolds off.

We should stop all of this right now, I thought, *just take our blindfolds off and not let ourselves get tied up like this.* But none of us did. Maybe we still felt powerful from the dance, or maybe we were full of ourselves. Maybe we were just plain scared of what the seniors would think of us if we quit. I didn't know. We just let them do it.

A girl, I was pretty sure she was Maggie, whispered to me as she tied my hand to another player, "If you can get out of this, all of your stuff is behind a big pine tree." *File that,* I thought to myself.

One of the seniors called out, "We'll be back in the morning, and you can get your cell phones then. Have a good night, freshmen." We could hear them move away and more cars start up and drive off.

Then it was quiet.

We knew we were alone and everyone started talking at once.

"It's so cold."

"I'm freezing."

"I want to go home."

Someone started to cry.

I heard Jules say, "Listen, we can get out of this if we work together."

Then Lindsay snapped at Jules, "You're so full of it, Jules. You always think you've got the answer. If it wasn't for you, we wouldn't even be here tonight."

We're in a mess. This is serious, and people are scared. Somebody needs to do something. Jules is the only one speaking up and no one is listening to her.

I tried to remember the coach's words, something about doubting shoes and digging down deep when things got bad. Well, we were sure in a tough situation now, and we had to get through it. *Think, think!*

I opened my mouth and kind of took charge. "Jules is right. We can do this. We're just not thinking it through. Jules, what did we bring that we have hidden in our sleeping bags? They have to be around here somewhere if we can just find them."

"We hid three flashlights, some water...."

"I brought six candy bars," somebody else said.

"Becky, is that you? It must be. No one else would think of food all the time."

That got us laughing, and then the comments started flying.

"I brought extra tampons just in case."

"That'll keep us warm."

"Stop it! You're making me laugh so hard I'm going to pee."

"Listen, you guys," I said. "I think I can find the sleeping bags if we can just get our blindfolds off."

"I've got a penknife in my back pocket." I recognized the husky voice. It was Sam.

"What, how come?" asked someone.

"Who cares? Who's next to Sam?" another girl said.

"I think I am," Kerry said. Kerry reached out. "Sam, is that you?"

"Yes," Sam said. "Reach into my left back pocket."

"I'm saying what I'm doing so you can all know what's going on," Kerry said. "I'm reaching now, and I have the knife."

Everyone cheered.

Kerry asked Sam to take the knife 'cause she was afraid of cutting herself. Sam gave us the play-by-play of her freeing Kerry's rope. It helped to know what was happening when we couldn't see. It was like keeping everyone in the game.

Once Kerry was freed, the rest of us became impatient because we all wanted to be next. I have to say, though, that we all listened to each other despite our anxiety. For once, we all wanted the same thing, and we needed each other to make it happen.

Within ten minutes, we all had our blindfolds off and we were just staring at each other in amazement. Here we were, in a clearing, in the middle of a wood, the whole team together, and we were totally dependent on each other.

"Let's find our stuff," I said.

We spread out but still stayed close to the clearing because it could have been easy to get lost. I didn't want them to know Maggie had told me where to find our things, so I pretended to search for a little bit before heading toward the back of a big evergreen tree. Sure enough, there were all the sleeping bags and coats in five oversized trash bags.

Well, this little clue of Maggie's will stay buried. No need to rat her out. She really did us a big favor.

"Over here, you guys," I called.

We were all cold, so we snatched up our coats, opened our sleeping bags, and wrapped ourselves up as best we could. We put all the trash bags into one and threw the blindfolds and rope in as well. We were keeping the evidence in case we wanted to use it later. Then we all huddled together to get warm.

"Look at what we just did working together," Becky said in amazement.

"We're not home yet," Lindsay said, still sounding peeved.

"Shut up, Lindsay," said Ellen. "One thing at a time."

"All right, what do we have?" I asked. "Who's got the flashlights?"

"I do," said Sam, followed by Anna and Steph.

We would need them to get out of the woods, and we were thankful they had brought them.

"We don't even know where we are. How will flash-lights help?" Heather wailed.

I said we might be on the east side of Route 206 since that was the only place left that had lots of undeveloped land. "The cars were on a dirt road before dumping us here. The dirt road has got to be close. If we follow it, it should lead us to a paved highway."

"Smart thinking, Jackie," said Lindsay. Then she turned to Jules. "I'm sorry. I shouldn't have said what I did to you. I was just freaking out."

"It's okay," said Jules. "Everyone was upset."

Anna, almost invisible in her dark green sleeping bag, suggested a plan to scout for the dirt road, and all of a sudden I was relieved of command. Everyone seemed to be getting on board with solving our problem. Three groups armed with the flashlights went out into the woods, trying to find the dirt road, while most of us remained in the clearing.

"So, does anyone want some of my candy bars?" Becky said.

We all laughed. "Me, me, me!"

Within five minutes, Jules' group found the dirt road. Tightly holding hands, we made our way down the half mile of dirt road until we came to the paved highway. Spotting a road marker, it was just what I had guessed. We were now on Route 206.

"Where are we? Which way do we go?" someone asked.

"Who knows this area?" Anna asked.

Sam thought it looked familiar and said that there was a gas station and a diner somewhere in the area, but she didn't know if they were to our left or right. Becky thought that lights from these businesses would make the sky seem lighter overhead, and we went with that idea. I had my fingers crossed the whole time 'cause I figured our little adventure wasn't over yet.

-22-

As we walked down the side of the road, cars occasionally passed us, but nobody stopped. After awhile, some of
girls started complaining that they were tired. Tori said we
might have better luck if she tried to hitch a ride by herself.
Jules wasn't going to let Tori go on her own 'cause there
were too many crazies out there, so we decided that Jules
would stay with the team and I would go with Tori.

Tori and I must have walked for about ten minutes,
trying to flag down cars, but no one stopped. Here we were,
two girls on a country road, and nobody was even slowing
down. You might have thought we were terrorists or
something. Finally, a large flatbed truck drove by and
eventually came to a stop fifty yards down the road. Tori and
I looked at each other, wondering if it was safe, and then
Tori got her courage up and said, "Let's go for it."

We jogged up to the truck's cab. A middle-aged man,
balding, wearing a Tennessee Titans sweatshirt that had seen
better days, leaned across the seat and rolled down the
window. "Why are you girls out on this country road? Don't
you know it's dangerous out here?"

We introduced ourselves and then blurted out our whole adventure, and the man looked at us in amazement.

"Where are the others?" he asked.

"Back there a little ways," Tori said.

"I can't back up the truck, the road's too narrow, but I'll wait until you go and get them. There's plenty of room in the back," the driver said.

Tori ran back while I waited, and soon our team started climbing in the truck, dragging their sleeping bags with them. When Tori climbed back into the truck's cab with me, the man introduced himself and said, "My name's Earl, and girls, this is a story I'm going to have to tell the boys when I get home. They're not going to believe I spent an evening with twenty-four young ladies all to myself." He gave us a wink.

About three miles down the road, we came to the Red Line Diner. "I can let all you gals out here. I'm going in for some coffee. Maybe one of you can call your parents from here. I'd let you use my cell, but it's broke and I haven't had a chance to get me another one yet."

"Don't worry about it. We appreciate everything you've done, Earl," I said, making a mental note to see if we had enough change between all of us to make a phone call from a public phone.

He slowly pulled his big truck into the parking lot. Then he said, "Tell you what, Miss Jackie. If you don't break the bank, I'll treat you gals to some coffee and Danish."

"That would be great," said Tori. "We'll pay you back. Just give us your address."

"Oh, that's okay. I think all you gals have earned it tonight," he said.

The team filled up one whole side of the diner. Our energy was almost back by the time the food arrived, and soon we were chatting away, the worst moments of the night starting to fade from our minds.

We all took turns thanking Earl. Heather called him our guardian angel, and I thought she was right. "We are going to dedicate our next game to you, Earl," said Tori.

"That would be mighty fine, young lady. No one has ever dedicated anything to me before."

Jules, Sam, Heather, and I were sitting together, trying to hatch a plan for what to do next. We decided that the less our parents knew, the better. Now that everyone was okay, we didn't want the hazing thing to get out, figuring it was something between us and the upperclassmen. Jules reminded us that we needed to get our cell phones back and get some sleep. She was right. We had a game tomorrow morning at eleven.

We decided to ask Earl if he would help us out one more time. If he could drop us off at Carly's house, we could get our cell phones and head to my house. This whole night could turn into a freshman team sleepover, and no one needed to know anything more than that.

Earl told us he didn't have a delivery and didn't have to be in New Brunswick 'til ten the next morning, so he agreed to take us to Carly's house to get our phones.

I collected some loose change from a couple of the girls and made the call to my house. When I talked to Dad, I didn't completely explain why we were leaving the senior's house. I only told him the team felt it would more fun "just being freshmen." I promised my dad that the girls would call their parents plenty early in the morning and that everyone would be up by 7:30.

We thanked Earl for the snacks and then piled back onto the truck. When Tori and I tried to figure out the directions to Carly's house, Earl said, "Give me her address. I got me a GPS. It can find anything."

Within fifteen minutes, we were at the house. Jules asked who wanted to come in with her.

I'll go," I said.

"Count me in," Tori said. "I don't want to miss this one."

The three of us marched up to the house with twenty-two sets of eyes watching right behind us. It took awhile for someone to answer the bell. Carly opened the door and stood there, speechless.

"Hi there," Jules said, real cool like. "We've come for our stuff."

Carly seemed frozen in place for a moment, but then she thawed, finally opening the door wider for us to come in.

In the basement recreation room, the other seniors were lounging around in cozy pajamas, sipping cocoa. Boy, the look on their faces was almost worth what we had gone through that night.

"What's going on?" asked Jill. It seemed like she was flustered and didn't quite know what to do.

"We decided we really didn't want to wait 'til morning to get our cell phones. We'll just pick them up now," Jules said.

"You weren't supposed to get away," another girl said.

"I guess we are a better team than you thought," Tori told them.

While Tori and I were gathering up the team's things, Jules turned to the seniors. "So here's the deal. None of our pictures ever show up on the internet. Make sure everyone knows that. What happened tonight is against school policy and you all know it, but we were trying to be good sports. You guys carried things way too far. You're lucky no one got hurt. Personally, I don't think very much of any of you, but the team agrees that as long as the pictures don't get out anywhere, we won't ever say anything about what you did. Got it?"

The seniors said okay, but they weren't too happy about it — except for Maggie, who had a little smile on her face. Having finished our job, we turned our backs on them and marched up the steps and out the door.

Ten minutes later, we were at my house. Mom and Dad took in our strange outfits and wild hair before they noticed a flatbed truck pulling away from the front of the house. They were trying to be cool and didn't say much, but they must have suspected something. I guessed they figured an explanation could wait 'til morning.

Having the team in the basement was kind of cool. We rolled out our sleeping bags, and after many trips to the bathroom, we finally settled down.

"You guys were great tonight," Anna said to no one in particular.

"I think that after tonight, there isn't anything we can't do as a team," Ellen said.

"I second that," said Caitlin, and others agreed.

"You know something? When things went wrong tonight, there was always a different person on the team who would pick us up," Heather said. "We just have to remember this night when we face the rest of our games this season."

It was a good point, but we were all too tired to think much about it. Everyone was yawning and mumbling goodnight. Most girls fell asleep right away. I was lying there thinking about what a night it had been. The most important part of all of it was that we were finally becoming a team.

I was starting to doze off when I heard someone sliding over to me.

"Jackie, you awake?"

It was Sam.

She whispered, "Jackie, I just want to say that I'm sorry about being such a jerk to you, hiding your stick and stuff. I don't know why, but sometimes if I'm not number one with everything, I feel like I'm a total loser. I don't know, maybe I was jealous or something. You're such a great player and scorer. I guess I'm not used to the competition."

Her words surprised me. And the part about my stick — jeez, I wanted to strangle her! I gave myself a moment before I said anything. Then I thought about the night and everything we had gone through. I needed to let the past go, but I knew I wasn't ready. I said the only thing I could.

"We both want to win, I know that, so maybe the only competing going on should be with the other team, Sam."

"You're right. It's something I need to work on."

I knew it took courage for her to speak up like that, so I said, "Sam, you were sure a great teammate tonight. I don't know what we would have done without your penknife and the flashlight."

I think she might have been smiling back when she said, "Night, Jackie. Thanks for hearing me out."

Lying there, I thought about our conversation and decided that the last piece of the puzzle, the answer to the problems between Sam and me, was resting with me now. Maybe it was my job to put it in place for all of us to be a real team.

In the morning, a lot of sleepy girls called their parents, and we discovered that my mom and dad had sent Matt out earlier to get juice and bagels for everyone. The next thing I knew, my kitchen and dining room were filled with twenty-three giggly, chatty girls. Lizzie was busy bouncing from one to another, loving the attention. Matt checked out the scene, shook his head, and went back up to bed.

After all the girls had been picked up, I wandered out into the kitchen. I thanked my parents and told them how much they had come through for me and the team.

"What happened, Jackie?" Mom asked. "I thought last night was supposed to be a big party for all the hockey players."

"I guess we figured out that the freshmen were a little too much for the varsity."

Mom looked at me, kind of confused. "You mean too many people were staying at the senior's house?"

"Something like that," I said hurriedly. "I better get upstairs and get a shower. We have a big game today."

As I started to leave the kitchen, I heard Dad say to Mom, "Anne, I don't buy Jackie's explanation for one minute. My gut tells me it was some sort of initiation that didn't quite go as planned. But it seems they found a way to work it out."

I knew that the morning's game would be the start of something good. We were plenty tired when the game got underway, but we played like there were more than eleven of us out on the field. It felt more like twenty-four.

We moved the ball like we knew what we were doing, and the defensive chatter got everyone pumped up. At the end of the game, which we won 2-0, Ms. O'Donnell told us that she was real proud of us and that it was the best she had ever seen us play. She said we looked like a real team, one that had played together for a long time. I thought she was right.

When we left the field, we were dragging, but at the same time, it seemed like we didn't want to let go of each other, like we were somehow connected. We knew we wouldn't forget what we'd been through together for a long, long time. Somehow, the evening had made us all tougher.

We also knew we were lucky to have gotten through the night with no one getting hurt. We decided that if hazing was a tradition at our school, it was a tradition that would die with us. That was for sure.

-23-

Tuesday we had a game with Henderson High, and when I got home, Mitch called. "How's the star?" he teased.

"You know I'm no star, but I'm psyched — the team is on fire!"

We talked about school stuff for a while and then he said, "Listen, I talked to Davey and he is calling Tori. Would you like to go to the movies Saturday night?"

"That would be great." I said. *Perfect.*

I wasn't sure if Dad remembered that he had already given his okay, so I decided to hit him up when he was in a good mood and looked for the right moment. Dad and Matt were already at the table having breakfast when I came down the next morning. Dad was deep in his sports page, as usual. Looking over his shoulder, I spotted that his favorite team had won.

"So Dad, on Saturday, Mitch, you remember him, you met him at the soccer game, well anyway, Tori and a boy named Davey are going to the movies, and Mitch asked me to go with him. Davey's dad will be dropping us off and Mitch's dad will bring us home. That's okay, right?"

"I guess so," Dad said slowly. I could see he was keeping back a grin, as if he had known all along who Mitch was and was just waiting out my long explanation. I wondered for a moment if he had done some sort of background check on Mitch to see if he was on the up and up, but I could have been mistaken about that.

Matt was listening, but he wisely decided to ignore my new social life. "I've got to get to school. You coming or not, Jackie?" It was the last thing he said to me, and we still rode to school pretty much in silence.

Mitch talked to me before world history about our date on Saturday. Then he said he hoped Matt and I had patched things up. I was amazed he even remembered, and I told Mitch how much I missed the old Matt.

While Mr. Coles was going on about Egypt, I thought about our conversation, and I wondered if Mitch missed his sisters and his mother. He must, but he never talked about it, and I didn't want to bring it up if it would make him feel bad or anything. At the end of the class, Mr. Coles announced a major history test for Monday, and as we left class, Mitch said, "Maybe we can study for the test together on Sunday."

"Maybe," I said, wondering, *wow, is that like a second date already?*

At lunch on Friday, I was finishing up my usual pizza when Jules reached into one of her books and handed me a note. "What's this?" I asked.

Jules laughed. "A message from my sister, the femme fatale. She wanted to discuss tomorrow night."

"What's tomorrow night?" Britt asked.

I blushed. "I'm going out is all. Someone from my class."

Lindsay got up from the table to throw away her trash. She turned to Jules and said, "Told you," and walked away laughing.

Saturday alternated between flying by and dragging. I had the house to myself for once since my parents had taken Lizzie with them to Matt's away game. I had begged off, saying I had too much schoolwork. After I finished, I was kind of proud of myself, but I was starting to feel fidgety about being with Mitch tonight.

After rifling through my closet, I called Tori for help. We decided I should wear my new chocolate brown sweater that had shirring on the sides and sleeves. I was going to pair it with my new matching jeans. That would make me look taller. At least, that's what Tori said.

I put all my clothes out on the bed and took a leisurely shower. It was almost five o'clock, and my parents were still not back yet. Mitch was supposed to be here at seven o'clock. I tried reading a few more pages of my latest English assignment, but I couldn't get into it. I was too hyped up, so I threw on some sweats and decided I'd get dressed after dinner. I was setting the table when my mom called. They were bringing home some hoagies and would be home in twenty minutes.

When my parents came in the door, I breathed a sigh of relief. Now that they were home, it seemed like the day was speeding up again, and that was a good thing. I had been thinking I was going to pass out with nerves, but now there was no more time to think because Mom and Dad were going on and on about Matt's game.

"They won 3-1," Dad said, and looking at my face, he said, "and no, he did not score, but he had two assists." I figured that meant Matt was probably starting to get his game back, and the thought made me smile. Maybe the worst was over for my brother.

"Where is Matt?"

"He's out with some of the other seniors. I think they said something about a party at one of the field hockey player's houses," Mom said. I wondered for a moment if that meant Maggie Brooks was on his radar screen. I hoped so.

"You look pretty excited. Big night tonight, huh?" Mom said.

"I think it will be fun to be out with Tori," I said between bites of hoagie.

"I'm sure," Mom said, laughing.

She knew she had me, that I was just trying to keep her from having any more ammunition. She was a smart one.

By 6:30, I was back upstairs getting dressed. After I put on some bronze lip gel that I thought would look good with my brown sweater, I decided to add some mascara. I probably didn't need it, but it **was** a date, and I figured a person was supposed to take everything up a notch.

My finishing touches were my grandma's gold and yellow topaz earrings that she had given me for my fourteenth birthday. I usually wore studs, but these earrings dangled, and I liked the way they felt against my neck when I moved.

I was ready, but I thought this date stuff was sure a whole lot of work. How did people get ready for something like a prom, anyway? It was beyond thinking. They probably needed a week off from school at least. I looked at myself in the mirror. I did look nice, kind of sparkly, but I really didn't think it was about the clothes. I was excited.

The doorbell rang, and I heard my dad's voice talking to Mitch. I went down the stairs just as my dad was introducing Mitch to my mom.

Mitch turned as he heard me coming, and the look on his face made me feel like Cinderella even without the fancy dress. "All set?" was all that he said.

"Yep. See you, Mom. See you, Dad." Then, just like that, we were out the door.

"Jackie," Mitch said softly, "you look terrific." I decided that maybe the mascara was a good idea after all, and more importantly, when he reached for my hand this time, I didn't pull away. I kept my hand in his all the way to the car.

Driving to the theater, Mitch and Davey started talking about the movie we were going to see, so I took the chance to really scope Mitch out. He was wearing black jeans, a gray T-shirt, and a black V-neck sweater. He looked so good, like someone from one of those preppy catalogues they had in the drugstore. How did I get so lucky?

Tori leaned over. "You look really nice, Jackie."

"You too," I said. She did, too, in her dark blue sweater dress. The girl could definitely dress.

There were a lot of kids at the theatre. Some were from Northfield and some were from our other local high school, St. Benedict's, and it looked like we were all heading to the same show. It was one of those horror pictures, you know, the kind that come out every fall when Halloween rolls around.

Sitting between Tori and Mitch, nothing on the screen was registering in my mind. I mean, if I ever had to do a book report on this movie, I would fail. Even with all that gore, all I could think about was Mitch sitting next to me in the dark.

At one point in the movie, there was a particularly creepy chase scene and Mitch put his arm around my shoulder. He smiled and said, "Just don't want the little lady to get scared." I knew that what he said sounded sort of corny, but it didn't matter. I liked it.

I smiled up at him. *This is perfect. No matter how many dates I go on in my life, I will never forget this night.*

As it got near the end of the movie, I knew this 'cause almost everybody in the film had been killed off, Mitch leaned over and whispered, "I really want to kiss you, Jackie McKendry, but not here." He just kind of touched his lips to the top of my head and my breath caught in my throat.

After the movie, we went across the street to a deli where the boys devoured two hoagies. Tori and I, who had only ordered sodas, looked at them in amazement.

"Do you always eat like this?" Tori asked Davey. "What about wrestling?"

"Mitch can, he's a growing boy, but believe me, I am going to enjoy these last two weeks because come October fifteenth, I have to start bringing my weight down. I'd like to be 152 or 145, but I might have to weigh in at 140," Davey said.

Just then, I heard a familiar voice. "Hi guys, how was the movie?" It was Ellen and her boyfriend, Danny Rucci, who was a sophomore at St. Benedict's. They had been to another movie in the theater where, Ellen said with a laugh, "Nobody died." We pulled up two more chairs and became a table of six. We spent the next hour talking about schools and sports, and before we realized how much time had passed, Mitch said we had to go.

Waiting for his father's car, I was thinking, *If this is dating, it's easier than I thought.* We weren't waiting long before a glistening black Tahoe pulled up to the curb and a tall hulk of a man got out and came over to us.

Mitch said, "Jackie, Tori, this is my dad, Major Kennedy. Dad, you know Davey."

"Glad to meet you, young ladies," his dad said, and he reached out his hand to greet us. If he was surprised at our firm handshakes, he kept it to himself. I got into the front of the car with Mitch while Tori and Davey sat in the back. It felt like I was sitting between two giants, and I sat up as straight as I could so I didn't just disappear.

Major Kennedy dropped Davey and Tori off at Tori's. As we pulled away from the Hanson's, Major Kennedy glanced at me and said, "I understand you're a bit of a feisty hockey player, Jackie."

I kind of blushed, but no one could see 'cause it was dark, thank goodness. "I try to help my team as best I can, sir."

"Well, that's good. When Mitch told me he had a date, I have to say, you are not what I expected."

"What *did* you expect?" I asked, his comment making me curious.

"Jackie, I am going to embarrass my boy, but back in Texas, those flirty cheerleader types were always fussing over him," he said, giving me a wink.

I knew he was playing, so I shot right back, "How come?"

His dad looked at me, threw his head back, and laughed out loud. "Mitch, you picked a winner."

"Yes sir, I know."

As we pulled up in front of my house, I asked Major Kennedy if he would like to come in and meet my parents. I had been thinking about this for a while. I figured Mitch's dad must be lonely without his family, so he might like to meet some other parents.

I introduced him to my mom and dad as Major Kennedy, but he corrected me and told them to call him Mike. That was when I knew I had done the right thing by asking him into our home. My parents invited him out into the kitchen for coffee. They asked Mitch and me to join them, but I said that we were going downstairs to play some pool instead.

Dad had partly finished the basement three years ago, and there were a ton of things for us kids to do. In the main room there was the pool table, of course, but also a dartboard, a small television, and a beat-up old sofa for lounging around with a coffee table in front of it loaded with games.

"This is great," Mitch said, looking around the room.

"It is. Matt has a lot of good times with his friends down here."

The rack for the pool cues was at the end of the room, and I started walking toward it. I was beginning to feel a little nervous finally being alone with Mitch, and the fun and easy part of the night seemed to be fading away. *Yikes, we're finally all alone. Will he try to kiss me? What if I'm not good at it? Will he think I'm stupid?*

He came up behind me, saying, "Thanks for inviting my dad in to meet your parents, Jackie. Most people wouldn't think of that."

Before I could turn around to answer, I felt his breath, his hands slid down my arms, and then his lips touched the back of my neck. The kiss made me feel all watery inside. He turned me to him and brought his hands up to my face, then slid his fingers through my hair.

"Reds, you're the best thing that has happened to me since I left Texas." He hesitated for a moment, trying to figure out something, like maybe if I wanted to be kissed. My face must have said yes because he slowly brought his lips to mine. *So soft*, I thought, and I found myself kissing him right back.

Then the kiss took itself up a notch. The room seemed to disappear; my thoughts went somewhere on vacation. After a few moments, I remembered my name and where I was. I brought my hands from his waist up to his chest and gently pushed myself away. I took a deep breath to steady myself, 'cause boy, oh, boy — and that's all I'm going to say about that.

Eventually, a few words of the English language came swimming back into my head, and I managed to say, "So, is this your way of stopping me from beating you at pool?"

He studied me for a bit, then grinned, and in a voice that seemed to have dropped an octave, he said, "Absolutely." He slowly moved away from me, chose a pool cue, turned with a wink and said, "Rack 'em."

We played for about half an hour, and each of us had a win. Major Kennedy called down, "Time to go, son."

Mitch gave me a quick kiss and jogged up the stairs. I turned off the lights and slowly followed him. Remembering the kissing, I think I could have floated up those stairs.

After the goodbyes, Dad turned to me and said, "I'm glad we met Mitch's dad. He seems like a good man. He certainly cares about Mitch."

He looked at me carefully. I was wondering if he somehow knew I had been kissed. Could a father really tell those things? But all he said was, "Did you have a good time tonight, honey?"

"The best, Dad. Simply the best."

-24-

Matt knocked on my door the next morning. He was acting differently, more like his old self, and then asked me if I wanted to go out for breakfast.

"Pancake House, my treat," he said.

"Sounds good to me. Give me five minutes," I said.

Driving to the restaurant, Matt said, "I'm sorry, kiddo, about the last few weeks. I know I've been a jerk. You were only trying to help, but I really didn't want to hear it. You know I have a thick skull. Some things just take awhile. Forgiven?"

I smiled and nodded.

"I miss Cheri, I can't deny it, but you were right. We are in two different places. I went out with the guys last night, and that helped. I forgot how much I had missed being with friends at my own school."

I wondered if one of those people was named Maggie. But I didn't want to chance asking. I'd been in his business enough. I was just so happy to have things all right between me and my brother I could barely stand it.

After the waitress took our order, Matt asked, "So, how was the big date with this Mitch character?"

"I had a great time."

"Do you really like him, Jackie, enough to get serious?"

"Maybe."

"Just take your time with this dating stuff. You're young yet."

I made a face at the young comment and he laughed. "Okay, okay. Just remember that if you need me, I'll be there. I mean it."

I smiled. I pictured a knight in shining armor galloping across a field, and I knew I would always think of my brother like that.

On our way home, I had a brainstorm. "Matt, Mitch and I talked about studying together. We both have a big world history test tomorrow. I was just thinking, maybe you could give me a ride to the library this afternoon. What do you think?"

"I think you have a sneaky little soul going on there, Jackie," he said, grinning. "Tell you what. I have some work that I could do at the library, too. If Dad says it's all right, I'll take you and bring you home. But your boyfriend has to get there on his own."

I ignored the boyfriend part and thanked him anyway. I wasn't really sure what you would call Mitch and me.

I phoned Mitch, and we agreed on a time and place to meet. When I explained to Dad that I wanted to meet Mitch at the library to study world history, he raised an eyebrow.

"Matt will be there the whole time," I pleaded, anticipating a negative rising in my dad's throat.

"Mitch seems like a nice boy," Dad said, "and it's fine if you go out and enjoy school activities together. But you are not going to be running around day and night making him the focus of your life. Is that clear?"

"Yes," I groaned. *Loud and clear.*

I went up to my room and changed into an olive sweat suit that was warm and comfy. I looked through my backpack to make sure I had everything. Checking the mirror, I thought, *See, Dad? I look serious about studying.* But I also knew I always got compliments on this outfit even though it was just sweats.

As we were walking into the library, Matt said, "I want to meet this guy." I was surprised. I told him I was supposed to meet Mitch at the information desk on the second floor, and when we got there, Mitch was already waiting.

I made the introductions, and Matt and Mitch shook hands, but I could see they were kind of eyeing each other up.

"Hey Jack, do me a favor. Go down to the car and get me my physics book. It's on the back seat," Matt said, flipping me his car keys.

I gave him a look, wondering why he couldn't get it himself. I remembered he did do me a favor bringing me here, though, so I played the obedient kid sister.

When I got back, I found Mitch and Matt still standing in the same place. They were both quiet, like something serious had gone on. It seemed kind of weird. I would have thought they would be talking up a storm about sports by now.

Matt sort of shuffled his feet and said, "I'll see you two later, let's say around 4:30 downstairs at the checkout desk," and he took off.

Mitch and I walked to the back of the library where there were some private study rooms. I asked, "Is something wrong?"

"No, everything's fine," he said. He put his books on the table, and we settled down on the low-slung chairs that were opposite each other.

I started to reach into my backpack, but Mitch said, "Jackie, wait." Then he slid his chair next to mine, turned to face me, and took my hands in his. I looked up and smiled.

"Your brother is a good guy, but a few minutes ago he threw a bucket of cold water over me, and…"

I was startled. *Whatever he says next, it will be something I'll remember for a long time.*

He hesitated before going on. "I just want you to know that you knocked me over from that first day in the auditorium when you jumped all over me for calling you Reds. Right then, I knew something was going to happen between us. Your brother told me that you haven't dated much, and he made it quite clear that I'm not to push you into anything you're not ready for. I want you to be my girlfriend, and for a long, long time. So, I'm just saying that we can take things slow and easy. Okay?"

I nodded my head slowly, trying to take in everything he was saying.

"Come here, Reds," he said, and he pulled me onto his lap and put his arms around me. "If you want to be my girl, I know I need to chill to make this work." He gave my curls a tug and grinned. "You don't have to worry. Your brother will kill me if I ever do anything to hurt you. I may be a few inches taller than him, but he has me by twenty pounds. If I mess things up with you, I could get pretty badly mangled."

Then his voice turned more serious. "So, Jackie, what do you think? Do you want to be my girl?"

I was blown away. I could never have imagined a conversation like this in a zillion years. I looked down at my hands resting in my lap, and then I slowly brought my hands up to his broad shoulders and risked saying what was in my heart.

"Matt's right. I watched him get badly hurt by a relationship that went way too fast, and I don't want that to happen to me. But I do feel happy when we're together. You're funny, and you understand how I feel about sports." I pulled my head back and smiled into his warm gray eyes. "And you're kind of cute, so yes, I'd like to be your girl. But Mitch, it's important that we're friends, too."

He smiled and gently kissed me. The kiss didn't last long, not like last night, but in a way it was better. I felt like we were like a team, in it together, and what we said to each other was more important than some big smoochie kiss.

He looked at me for a while, taking in what I said, I guessed. Then he kissed my knuckles, smiled, and said, "Now that we've got the big stuff settled, you better get off my lap, girlfriend, and stop distracting me from my work."

I slid over to the opposite chair, and I was pretty sure there was a gigantic grin on my face when I said, "Okay, chapter three, *Cultures of the Nile Valley.*"

At 4:15, we packed up to go downstairs and Mitch said, "I'm glad we talked."

I smiled up at him, and I thought about everything that would have passed me by if I had not said yes to what was in my heart.

-25-

While I was drying my hair on Monday morning, I played the whole weekend in my mind. I never thought things would turn out the way they did. I mean, I actually had a boyfriend now. And despite his teasing and all, there was something about Mitch that made the idea of us being together a very comfortable one. It was as though I didn't have to be anybody else for him to be interested in me. I liked that part the best.

At lunch, the girls could not wait to get my version of things. I mean, it was pounce city. I laughed at their questions, then turned the tables and asked Jules, "What did Tori say?"

"Tori had a good time."

Lindsay wasn't having any of my evasiveness. "So, Jackie, is he as hot as he looks?" she asked, a wicked expression on her face, ready for some juicy gossip.

I could feel my face grow warm, I couldn't help it, but I wasn't going to give her anything. "Gee, I have nothing to compare it with. Ask me again after I've dated the rest of the freshman class," I said with a serious face.

"Good one, Jackie," Alisha said, and both Jules and Lindsay howled at that 'cause they knew that it was **so** not me.

In world history, I was surprised that the test on ancient Egypt was so easy. I thought I got most of the answers right. Having Mitch to study with was a huge help. Sometimes, guys can be a good influence.

The week was flying by; two more games became two more wins for our team. On Wednesday, Mitch had his first student council meeting. When he called me that night, he said it was great to meet the other eighteen class representatives and see the class officers in action. He said Alicia did a great job, which was no surprise to me.

Thursday, during physical education class, Mrs. Fortunato gave me a hall pass and asked me to take a note down to the main office. "Can I go like this?" I asked, looking down at my navy gym shorts and white T-shirt.

"It's not a problem. Just be back before the class is over."

I left the note at the office and wandered down a different hallway 'cause I wasn't in a rush to get back for badminton. Halfway down the hall, I thought I saw Mitch standing outside a classroom door, talking to some girl. He didn't see me. I felt funny, like maybe I caught him out.

I quickly turned and walked away. My heart was lurching. That girl was really leaning awfully close to him, or maybe he was leaning into her. Doubts about Mitch and me seeped into my mind. Maybe he didn't mean the things he said this weekend. He really could have any girl he wanted.

I turned the corner, walked a few more steps, and stopped. *What am I doing? He asked me out. He calls me at night. Mom said you have to trust your heart.* I took a breath, grabbed a hold of some McKendry spirit, and walked back the way I had come.

They were still there. As I got closer, Mitch, still with his back to me, took a step toward the door, and now I saw that the second person was Emma Connors. Her eyes were glued right on Mitch. She looked like a vulture ready to swoop down on her prey.

I overheard him say, "A freshman dance is a great idea. I think my girlfriend will love it."

"Oh," Emma said. I was a few steps away. "I thought you were a free man. Somebody here at Northfield?" she asked sweetly.

I had almost reached them when a little devil inside me made me do something I never thought I would do. I walked right up to Mitch, put my arm around his waist, and smiled up at him. Then, without missing a beat, I looked Emma Connors right in the eye.

"Hi, Emma," I said. Emma looked shocked for an instant, as if she couldn't believe what she was seeing. She quickly hid her reaction, but I caught it just the same.

Mitch turned and smiled, then immediately put his arm around my shoulders and gave me a hug. "Hi, babe." He grinned and took a long, slow look at my T-shirt and shorts. And then his eyes kept traveling slowly down the length of my legs. "Nice...outfit!"

I blushed as I smiled up at him. "I don't want to interrupt your conversation; I have to get back to the gym. See you later, Mitch." I waved a hand at both of them, my face all innocent like.

I was grinning mischievously all the way back to the gym. For a moment, I felt like I might have made an enemy in Emma Connors, but I didn't care. I realized that deep inside, when I really wanted something, I could go for it, and sometimes being number one in love was awfully sweet.

-26-

On Friday night, Mitch and I planned to go to my brother's soccer game. His dad dropped him off at my house, and my parents would take him home after the game. It was going to be an important night for Matt since two scouts were coming to the game.

When Mitch arrived, I could feel the cold air rush in behind him. He was wearing a down jacket that was Northfield navy blue. The color made his gray eyes look even darker, and I thought again how good looking he was. He gave me a quick kiss and I led him out to the kitchen.

"How was open gym?" I asked as we sat down at the kitchen table.

"It's going great. I'm really anxious for the season to start."

"I bet. I'm glad hockey comes in the fall and I don't have to wait."

Mitch started drumming his fingers on the table. I could tell that something was on his mind. Finally, he stopped. "Jackie, listen. Once basketball begins, it gets kind of crazy.

193

Sometimes we practice at night and sometimes in the afternoon," he said, sounding a little wound up. "I probably won't have the free time for us like I do right now. I don't want it to mess things up for us."

I started to say something, but Lizzie came out to the kitchen and gave Mitch a big hug. I watched my sister trying to worm her way around Mitch, making the moment all about her. She asked him how he liked her new coat, and I chuckled. *She is definitely going to drive Mom and Dad crazy someday.*

"All ready?" Dad asked when he joined us in the kitchen. I grabbed my parka and gloves from the hall closet and we headed out to the car.

In the back seat of the car, I reached out and gave Mitch's hand a squeeze, and he seemed to relax a little. Soon the five of us were settled in to watch Matt's game. It was funny; it didn't seem so bad sitting with my family tonight when I had Mitch next to me.

Just before the start of the game, the scout from Drexel, who was actually their assistant coach, introduced himself to my parents. When he started talking with them, I noticed Mitch perk up. *He's really interested in this recruiting stuff. I wonder if Mitch expects to play college basketball. Just how good is he?* I was kind of curious about that. In all this time, I had never seen him play, not even fooling around.

At halftime, Mitch and I decided to get some hot chocolate at the refreshment stand. Lizzie made a pleading face so I knew we couldn't come back empty handed. As we got around the back of the bleachers and were out of the glare of the lights, I took Mitch by surprise, stopping and wrapping my arms around his waist.

"Remember in the library, when you said we would take our time?" I asked. He nodded, and I went on. "If you love basketball as much as I love hockey, then everything will be okay. We'll find a way to be together, don't worry. I want you to give basketball a hundred percent. I never want anything to get in the way of how either of us feels about sports."

"Thanks, Jackie. That means a lot," he said as he pulled me even closer, wrapping his long arms around me and giving me a hug.

I pulled away, grabbed his hand, and said with a grin, "Besides, who says you won't get cut?" He laughed, shaking his head all the way to the refreshment stand.

As we watched the second half, I was really excited by how Matt was playing. *Who could not want him on their team?*

Mitch whispered to me, "He's doing great out there. What other school is coming tonight?"

"I think a coach from Delaware."

"Well, the more people who see you, the better," said Mitch.

"Do you know a lot about that stuff?"

"A little. My dad has always talked about sports. He kept me out of first grade for a year. He thought I would have a better chance at competing in sports if I was a little older. I'll be sixteen in April, and I should really be a sophomore."

"Do you feel pressured to play basketball?" I asked, thinking of Chris Hanson.

"Oh, no, nothing like that, it's just an option, but Jackie, I love basketball. When I am on the court, there is nothing else. I feel like, I don't know, like I'm the real me out there."

I smiled. "I definitely know what you mean."

In the following week, the hockey team remained undefeated, with a win and a hard-fought tie. Two starters were out with the flu for that game, so we were lucky to escape without a loss. The early season tie was the only other blemish on our record.

We were now 10-0-2 and in first place in our conference. Ms. O'Donnell told us that the top three teams would have a chance to play for the freshman conference championship. We had a bye while the second and third place teams had to play each other for the right to face our team next Tuesday.

With that news, the whole team was motivated to step it up another notch. We were pumped every day to come to practice. Becky was now our number one goalkeeper, and she looked great. Kerry acted as positive as ever, and the two goalkeepers seemed to get along well in practice. But if it was me, I wasn't so sure I would've had it in me to be that upbeat if I were replaced.

And the thing with me and Sam...I'd say it was mostly a truce. She didn't try to do me in, and I tried to keep our history on the back burner. For now, all eyes were on the prize.

-27-

On Thursday night, Tori called me all excited. "Our father has relented! He's going to let us have a party. Jules and I have been bugging him for weeks, but we didn't want to say anything until he gave the official okay."

"What kind of party will it be? Who will you ask?" I wanted to know.

"Daddy wanted to keep it small, you know, maybe only twenty people. But Jules and I couldn't figure how we could invite some of the girls from the team and not others. It would be different if we weren't in season."

"So what are you going to do?"

"Well, we were going to ask just the team, but I say, what's a party without boys? So, Jules and I made a list. Besides the team, there is Britt, Alisha, and the two K's. That makes twenty-eight girls. Now, for the boys, there's Davey of course and Mitch, and then there is Kurt, Will, Ellen's boyfriend Danny, Tom, Bryan, Adam Zigler..."

"I didn't know you knew Adam Zigler," I said.

"Well, I don't. Jules wants to invite him. I think he is in some of her classes. Some of the girls might want to bring a date, too. Heather is going with that sophomore, what's his name, Kent? But I definitely need to keep control of the list. Daddy says the girls have to tell me if they are bringing someone."

"Is your brother going to be there?" I asked, thinking that would make a lot of girls very happy.

"He's going to be an extra chaperone, along with four other guys from St. Benedict's team. Since Daddy is their coach, they'll do a good job. They'll also make sure nobody tries to crash the party."

"That's a great idea."

"Oh, Daddy knows all about teenagers and parties, and he'll be particular about who he asks from his team to work it. Some of his players would cause more trouble than the people we invite to the party, and he's not about to allow anything to go wrong at his own house."

I pictured some of the teenage parties I had seen in movies and how they had gotten out of hand with kids wrecking the place. The idea that it could ever happen at the Hanson's was almost a laugh.

"We're going to have it the Saturday after Halloween," Tori said.

"Is it a Halloween party then?"

"We thought about it. We'll decorate that way, but no costumes. We want it to be pretty casual."

"I'm excited, Tori, it sounds like so much fun."

"Yeah, we're going to invite the girls tomorrow."

Tori and Jules issued their invitations after practice. Most of the girls seemed pretty excited, but as I looked around, I thought that some of the girls were just pretending. Like, when it came down to it, they just didn't want to go to a boy/girl party.

If this had happened two months ago, I might have felt the same. Maybe it was tricky business to mix your sports friends with your social friends in high school. I guessed that as long as we were a team on the field and respected each other's feelings off the field, it would be enough for everybody. You know, like everyone walking their own path kind of thing. At least, I hoped so.

I told Mitch about the party that night. "So, are you asking me as your date or just telling me about the party so I can be jealous of whoever you invite?" he asked.

I laughed. "Mr. Kennedy, will you be my date at the Hanson Halloween party?"

"It will be my honor, Ms. McKendry. Seriously, it sounds like a lot of fun."

The next week was a big week for both Mitch and me. When we talked, we weren't sure who was more nervous, me for my championship game on Tuesday or Mitch for basketball tryouts on Thursday. We both hoped we would have a lot to celebrate at Saturday's party.

-28-

On Tuesday morning, I woke before the alarm even went off and jumped right out of bed. I peeked through the window blinds and thought, *Good, no rain; today will be the day we win the championship.*

Because we were the higher seeded team, the game would be played at Northfield, which meant we got to wear our home uniforms. What was even better was that we'd be playing on the varsity field, which was still in really good shape.

I made sure I had everything, rechecking my list, before I headed down to breakfast. Everyone wished me luck, and both Mom and Dad said they'd see me at the game.

We were all wired at lunch. Lindsay couldn't keep her leg still, and Britt yelled at Lindsay for almost spilling her milk. Jules was unusually quiet and distracted. When I asked her what she was thinking about, she said, "Too much. I need to calm down."

"Everyone does," I said. "Remember what we have gone through this freshman season? How could any team face the things that we did together?" Lindsay and Jules just looked at me and then glanced at each other.

"You're right, Jack. We're going to do it," Lindsay said, giving me one of her rare smiles.

Lindsay's leg stopped jiggling, and Britt looked over to me and said, "Thanks, Jackie, I can finally have my lunch in peace." We all laughed.

There were a bunch of people at the game, more than usual. A lot of parents from both teams had come as well as some of our freshman friends. It turned out that we were facing the team we had tied early in the season, New Gretna. It was the team with the awesome goalkeeper.

The game was intense from the opening whistle, and I thought, *This sure isn't the team we played before.* They had gotten a lot better. Both teams battled hard in the midfield, but neither team could get much in the way of scoring opportunities.

After a great halftime speech by Ms. O'Donnell, our team came out fired up in the second half. We started putting more pressure on the New Gretna defense, and we were able to get off some good shots on goal. But it seemed that the more shots we took, the better the New Gretna goalkeeper played.

With four minutes left in the game, the New Gretna goalie dove for a ball, and Sam was right on it. The goalkeeper quickly covered the ball with her hand, which was a major no-no in hockey, and the whistle blew for a penalty stroke. Ms. O'Donnell called from the sidelines, "Jules, take it."

Both teams stood behind the twenty-five yard line, waiting for the stroke to take place. It could have been the game right there. On the referee's whistle, Jules put the ball high toward the right-hand post, but the goalkeeper was able to get her glove on it, and at the last second, she was able to tip it away. No score. After play started up, both teams fought back and forth as the clock ticked down.

With just over a minute left, Tori intercepted a ball at the defending forty yard line. She quickly sent an outlet pass to Sam, who took off down the field. Sam dodged one defender and was nearing the striking circle.

Does she see me here on the outside or is she going to take it herself? I wondered. The New Gretna goalie started to go out on Sam, and just when I thought Sam was going to shoot, she faked right, pulling the goalkeeper with her, and slipped the ball to me as I was coming in on her left.

Now there was just me and an open cage. I touched the ball with my stick, and as I brought my stick back to slap it into the cage, I heard pounding footsteps behind me. My stick started to move into the ball for the shot, but a New Gretna defender came out of nowhere and sent me sprawling to the ground. My head slammed into the goalpost, and for a moment, there was nothing.

The ball must have rolled out of bounds 'cause I heard a whistle, and somebody was saying penalty stroke. Sam was leaning over me. "Jackie, Jackie, are you okay?"

"What?" I said, feeling kind of woozy. I started to get up, but my legs were shaky.

Finally, I stood. The ref asked me if I was all right. "I think so," I said.

The ref asked if I was going to take the stroke. *The perfect moment, just like in my dream,* but then I thought a little more. *No, not this time. I know I'm too wobbly.*

I looked at Sam, who had her arm around me, and I slid the last piece of the puzzle firmly in place, saying, "Sam, can you do it for me instead?"

Sam looked me in the eye, and when she spoke, I could hear the steel in her voice. "Yeah, Jackie, I will."

As the team backed away to the twenty-five yard line, Ms. O'Donnell asked me if I was okay and I waved that I was. She asked me if I wanted to take the stroke, but I said no, I thought Sam should take it.

Everyone was quiet; this might be our final chance. Both teams were holding the hands of their teammates, waiting. The referee blew her whistle, and Sam flicked a low rocket into the left-hand corner of the cage. The goalie had no chance. Goal! I could feel the heat of excitement. Every nerve ending was firing, but I knew it was still too soon to celebrate.

We headed back to the center for the start up, and I heard the New Gretna players call over to their coach, "How much time is left?"

"Forty seconds," their coach yelled. "You can do it."

Well, they could have, against some other team at some other time, but not that day.

Our Northfield freshman team was not letting anything get through them, around them, or over them. We could hear our teammates on the bench screaming and yelling. The person on the clock was counting down, "Four, three, two, one, zero." The whistle blew.

Pandemonium broke out as players ran onto the field. Everyone was hugging and crying. Ms. O'Donnell came up to Sam and put her arm around Sam's shoulder. I overheard her say, "Sam, I'm so proud of you."

Sam smiled back. "Yeah, Coach, the stroke."

"No, Sam," Ms. O'Donnell said. "The stroke was great, but I'm talking about the pass to Jackie. You really became a hockey player to be proud of today."

After the celebration on the field wound down and we were all saying our goodbyes, I slowly made my way through the crowd toward my parents' car. I didn't really want to leave. It seemed like such a magic place right at that moment.

"Look who's here, Jackie," Mom called out.

I perked up. It was Mitch and his dad. They had come to the game, and now they were going to join us for dinner, which made it all just about perfect.

We went to my favorite Italian restaurant. After we were seated, Mitch said to me, "Congratulations. It was an awesome game."

"I'm glad you could see it. I'm **so** happy right now."

I looked into his beautiful gray eyes and wondered how anyone's freshman season could end more perfectly than mine.

"So how did you like the game, Major Kennedy?" I asked, wondering if he was into the game at all.

"Jackie, that was sure exciting; I have never seen a field hockey game before. You girls work really hard, and I was impressed by the way you all communicate on the field. If you were in the service, I would say that your team would have made a fine fighting unit, one that anyone could be proud to have by their side."

I grinned, and Mitch said, "Dad thinks of everything in terms of the military."

"No, I get it, Mitch. You're right, Major Kennedy. Today we were all together for sure."

As my parents and Major Kennedy became wrapped up in some adult conversation, Mitch and I had a chance to talk.

"I never asked you," Mitch said. "How was that sleep-over your team had with the upperclassmen? Your mom said everybody ended up at your house. Weren't you supposed to go somewhere else?"

I just smiled at him through my exhaustion. "We did for a while, and then there was a change of plans. Someday, maybe I can tell you all about it."

Mitch reached under the table and took my hand. He leaned toward me and said in a low voice, "I like it when you say someday, Jackie McKendry."

Epilogue

It's June and it looks beautiful outside. I quietly slip out the back door so I won't wake anyone. I re-tie my shoes, adjust my iPod, and breathe in the cool stillness in the air. It's perfect for my Saturday morning run.

I can't believe that freshman year is almost over. Matt will be graduating in three days, and he will soon be busy working soccer camps and getting ready for college. I know he's looking forward to what is coming next in his life. In January, he finally narrowed his college search and accepted an athletic scholarship to a university within an hour and a half from our home.

The school has a winning soccer program, and when Matt visited, he felt really comfortable with the guys on the team. He also likes the school's co-op program for business students. He confided in me that part of his choice was based on the fact that Mom and Dad could come to his games.

I begin my warm up jog for the three-mile run. Of course, it will end at my favorite lookout on the hill. I'm glad I took the time to be alone this morning. I feel like a stage in my life is ending; soon, I won't be a little freshman anymore.

I get the sense that a new chapter is waiting in the wings, ready to be written, just like the book I thought about so long ago.

I cross the street and turn down Brandywine Drive, thinking about the new friends I made, the team, and the adventures we experienced together. We discovered so much about what it took to be on a successful team. Ms. O'Donnell sure played a big part in that, too. I'll miss her. I sure hope that we can take what we learned and use it this fall when we're sophomores.

There was something magical about our team once we all decided to play together. I know that not every team gets to feel that. Even though they had an 18-3 record, the varsity girls fell short of going all the way. They were devastated when their season ended.

Matt's girlfriend, Maggie Brooks, who Mom actually likes, told me all about it. She said that the team couldn't seem to put aside the petty squabbling for the benefit of achieving the one goal they said they all wanted.

As I finish my first mile, I check my watch, pick up my pace, and start thinking about the people who had come through my life this year. Some had drifted away, like the two K's, and I think that not all twenty-four of us freshmen will be staying with the team come September, either.

Maybe that's what growing up is about sometimes, beginnings and endings. Lindsay was right — nothing stays the same, and that can be a sad thing. But maybe it's what needs to happen. Maybe we have to shed part of ourselves, kind of like a snake sheds its skin, to become the thing we were meant to be. Just the same, growing up isn't easy, not when you're in the middle of it.

One thing that has remained the same this year is how I feel about Mitch. I smile whenever I think about him. My first date and my first real kiss — I'll remember them forever. I look down at my wrist and see the copper and beaded bracelet gleaming in the sun. It's my first gift from a boy I truly like.

It was Christmas Eve when he had surprised me with it. He and his dad were having dinner with my family. It turns out that his mother is a jewelry designer, and she made it especially for me. It arrived right before Christmas, and Mitch confessed he had been really nervous that he wouldn't get it in time. Looking at it now, I love the special way his mother mixed the garnet and amber beads into the copper. I know I will always treasure it.

For my part, I gave Mitch a copy of Charley Rosen's *The House of Moses All-Stars*, a basketball story that he devoured. I had to search and search the bookstore. It was so frustrating when I saw all the books in the sports section. I finally went up to a sales clerk and told him what Mitch was like, and he helped me find just the right book.

The winter was like Mitch said it would be: almost all basketball. I remember the first time I saw him play. He finally came off the bench several games into the varsity season, and he never sat again. I have to laugh now, remembering that I wondered if he was any good. I don't play basketball myself, but I know enough about sports to say his talent is very special.

In a few days, Mitch will be flying home to Texas, and he won't return 'til the end of August. I hate the idea of him not being around this summer, but I know that my friends and family will keep me plenty busy.

I'm looking forward to training with Mrs. Fortunato and learning more about field hockey from this amazing coach. Some of the other freshmen and I have already signed up for hockey camp with the upperclassmen.

As I start up the long hill, what I realize most is that I'm no longer the person I was in eighth grade. My friends and I, all of us, have grown and changed. There was Alisha putting herself out in front of our whole class, Jules standing up to the upperclassmen, Anna walking away from the team she knew to reach out to her new team. Even Sam Jones admitting she had been wrong was a big deal. In my own way, I took risks too, trying more in school and speaking up when the team really needed someone. Maybe the most important risk was taking a chance with my heart.

I wonder if things will be this perfect next fall. When Mitch comes back, will he still be my boyfriend or will he find somebody new? Then I think about the returning upperclassmen and how they'll treat us freshmen. Will it be any kind of team when we're finally all together on the same field?

But that's the future. Right now, I have today, and my goal. I smile and pick up my pace to get to the top of that hill.

The End

Acknowledgments

It can be a daunting task to shift careers, but my journey into writing has been made easier by the support of great people in my life. Many thanks to my readers for their suggestions — Barbara Thompson, Kat Rowland, Beth McGinnis, Jennifer Marino, Tricia Marino, MacKenzie McGuckin, and Carling Mott. A special shout out goes to the Mt. Holly Writers Group for suffering through my first attempts, especially Diane Fretz and Jim O'Brien. Thanks to the North Wildwood Writers Conference and the folks at Infinity Publishing for this opportunity to share my characters and their story to my readers. Lastly, I would like to thank my other half, who endured countless hours without my company while I was holed up in the blue room, bent over my computer, writing this story.